<u>Her Knight in Street King Armor 2</u>

<u>The Grim & Kaliyah Love Story</u>

By Kelly Marie

Previously

Kaliyah Diamond

*T*HE FEELING OF SOMETHING COLD *and hard touching my skin woke me out of my sleep. I opened my eyes to see Goldie standing in my room with a knife pressed into my neck, almost breaking my skin.*

"What are you doing?"

"Shut the fuck up!" she snapped quietly.

"Did you really believe I was going to be okay with you fucking Grim?" she asked, and I swallowed hard.

"Bitch, you got me all the way fucked up! I should have beaten your ass the second you walked into this house, but I slept on you and now I'm paying for it," she continued as she pressed the knife, and I gasped. This was the third time I woke up to somebody in my room who wanted to cause me harm. I should have felt fear, but I didn't. I felt rage... pure rage from everything that I had ever gone through, all the times people wanted to hurt me, and all the things that were done to me. Deshaun's words danced around in my head... "stand up for yourself". I could hear it clearly as if he was standing there saying it to me.

She grabbed my hair, causing my head to snap back and expose more of my neck.

"Bitch, who told you that you could fuck my man?"

"He said you two were not together... and I love him," I finally admitted.

"You love him? What the fuck would your little ass know about love, huh? Did you give him six fucking years of your life, bitch?" she snarled in my face.

"No! Bitch, you didn't. I fucking did! He should be mine... he is mine, and I would rather kill your ass than allow you to walk away with him. I love him... not you!"

She yanked my hair.

"I don't know where the fuck you came from, and I could care less, but you better go back, and leave my fucking man alone, or I'm about to gut your ass like a fish, bitch."
"I don't have anywhere else to go." I tried to loosen her grip on my hair. "I don't fucking care!"

She shook me and tightened her grip on my hair.

"You should have thought of that before you sat on his dick. How dare you fuck my nigga!" she said before releasing my hair and striking me in the face, busting my lip on impact. I tried to cover my face, but she was still able to hit me a few times in the face.

No matter what I did, she kept on raining blow after blow to my face. Unable to take any more, I snapped and sent a fist straight into her face. She stumbled back a little, giving me enough time to jump off the bed and swing on her again.

She was bigger than I was and dragged me like a rag doll, yet I continued to fight. At some point, she dropped the knife, and we crashed all over the room as we were entangled in a blur of arms, legs, and her weave flying about. I sensed when the lights turned on, but I couldn't see anything, because my hair was all over my face, and blood was seeping into my right eye.

"Goldie, let her the fuck go, now!" I heard Deshaun's voice echo in the room. I felt his hands trying to separate us, but the more he pulled at her, the tighter she gripped my hair. I continued to swing, hoping to get free. I could feel Deshaun pulling on her. She lost her grip on me, and I lost my balance, falling on my ass. As I flew back and landed on the floor, I felt the handle of the knife brush against my hand. At that point, I didn't see Goldie. I saw my mama, Zoe, my uncle, and Silvan attacking me and doing all kinds of things to me.

"JUST LEAVE ME ALONE!" I screamed and ran toward her while swinging. Deshaun jumped in front of me to stop me, but somehow, in this tiny body, I found the strength to push on. I pushed through him to get to her. I saw nothing and no one but her! She was the image of all my pain and suffering, and I wanted her. I closed my eyes and let my rage take over like a wave rushing over me.

"Oh my God! What did you do?" she suddenly screamed at me, but I didn't care. She deserved everything that I was about to unleash. I was sick and tired of being sick and tired. I was no longer going to be that weak Kaliyah who everybody targeted. I was fighting back!

"Kaliyah..."

Deshaun's voice suddenly calling out to me calmed down my rage and thoughts. Instantly, I stopped my rampage and focused on his voice, opening my eyes, but when I did open them, I couldn't believe what I saw. Deshaun was on his knees, looking up at me with a knife plunged into his stomach.

"Oh my God. What... did I..." I panicked and looked down at my hands that were covered in his blood. I stabbed him! I had

stabbed Deshaun! I didn't even remember picking up the knife. I just blacked out! Tears fell from my eyes as I looked down at him. He tried to reach out to me but fell back and closed his eyes.

"YOU KILLED HIM!"

She pushed me and screamed at me, but I couldn't function because of what was happening around me. All my eyes saw was Deshaun lying in a pool of his blood. What did I do?

Chapter One

Kaliyah Diamond

I COULD BARELY SEE from all the tears that were flowing from my eyes, but I knew in my heart that I had killed him. Goldie continued to scream and cry, but I blocked her out. I felt Deshaun's face, hoping that he would open his eyes for me, but he didn't even flinch, and his skin felt cold.

"I'm so sorry!" I cried out with my head back as my heart ripped to pieces.

"What the fuck? I hate you so fucking much!" Goldie yelled at me and grabbed me. I pushed her hands off and looked back at Deshaun. His blood was just running out of him as he laid motionless on the floor. I noticed his phone next to him. It must have fallen when he tried to stop me and Goldie from fighting. I grabbed it and unlocked it since he had given me the code to use it whenever I wanted to text Pedra.

"What the fuck are you doing? You can't call the cops!" Goldie yelled at me, but I ignored her. I scrolled to Optimus' name and called his number.

"Yo, G," he answered almost immediately.

"HELP ME, OPTIMUS!" I screamed with all the strength I had left. "Aye, what the fuck is going on, Kaliyah?"

"It's Deshaun! I... I think he's dead! Please help me, Optimus! I don't know what to do."

"KALIYAH WHAT THE FUCK ARE YOU TALKING ABOUT? WHERE THE FUCK YOU AT?" his deep voice roared through the phone.

"We are at his house, and he's… he's been stabbed," I said. The line went silent, but I knew he was still there. I could hear him breathing.

"We're on our way! Check that he's breathing, and get something to hold pressure on the wound."

"Okay," I answered.

"FUCK! We're on the fucking way!" he shouted before hanging up in my face. I rushed to my dresser and grabbed a towel. Heading back to Deshaun, I dropped to my knees and cradled his head.

"What… what are you doing?" Goldie sniffled after her meltdown finally stopped.

"Deshaun?" I called him as I held the towel on his wound and applied pressure. I leaned down, planted a soft kiss on his lips, and rested my head on his.

"I'm so sorry, baby. I'm sorry," I said as my tears fell and dropped onto his face.

"You better not kiss him again, bitch. This is all your fault," Goldie said, and I looked up at her with all the hate I ever felt pulsating through my veins. I didn't understand how this was solely my fault when she was the one who came into my room with a knife!

She must have felt what I was truly feeling, because her face softened, and she backed up away from me. I turned my attention back to Deshaun and cradled his head. I must have been sitting there forever, because next thing I knew, Optimus and Goliath came crashing into the room.

"WHAT THE FUCK HAPPENED?" Optimus growled,

dropping to his knees.

"I… it was an accident," I stuttered.

"She happened!" Goldie shouted, pointing at me after finally finding her backbone since they were now in the room. Both Goliath and Optimus looked at me with stares that made my blood run cold.

"I wasn't trying to hurt him. I was fighting with Goldie, and he got in the way—"

"You stabbed him, bitch! Stop fucking lying!" she yelled, cutting me off. "NO, I DIDN'T, GOLDIE! YOU STARTED THIS!"

"Who is the one with the fucking blood on her hands?" she asked as she pointed at my hands.

"Both of you bitches shut the fuck up! I don't care about either of y'all right now, but you better pray to whoever you pray to, Kaliyah, that my man ain't dead, or I promise I'm going to fucking kill you myself!" Optimus said as he and Goliath lifted Deshaun off the floor. I looked at him to see if there was any hint of a lie in his eyes, but I didn't find any, so I knew that he would kill me.

After glaring at me with so much hatred in his eyes, he turned away from me and they rushed out of the room with Goldie right behind them. I sat on my knees on the floor and closed my eyes. I tried to piece together what happened and how I ended up stabbing him.

I didn't even remember picking up the knife. This was all my fault. This was the only man who had truly cared for me and helped me, and I killed him. I sat on the floor and cried until I passed out.

Chapter Two

Goldie Lawson

"GRIM... I'M HERE, BABY. Please be okay!" I cried in the back of Optimus' car as we rushed to New York Presbyterian Brooklyn Methodist Hospital at 506, 6th Street.

"Goldie, shut the fuck up!" Optimus yelled at me, and I looked up at him through the rearview mirror. He flicked his eyes at me and gave me a cold scowl.
"Why are you talking to me like that?" I dropped my hands on my hips.

"Because we all fucking know you had something to do with this! That girl wouldn't just stab him like that. Tell me... why the fuck she would do that?" he asked, and I had no answer for him. How the fuck would he know? He wasn't even there. I looked down at Grim and guilt fell over me as I replayed what happened in my head.

Kaliyah was swinging at me and had the knife in her hand. It was like she morphed into the miniature Incredible Hulk, because Grim was barely able to keep her away from me, and for the first time, I was afraid. My back was pressed against the dresser, and only Grim's body was between her and me. I thought about hitting her with something from off her dresser, but she didn't have anything on it but lotion.

I was hopeful that Grim would gain control over her, but then, he ripped my heart out when he called her baby... BABY! I was always just Goldie, even when we fucked. He was always quiet in the bedroom and hardly moaned, but I would be so vocal, calling him all kinds of daddy and baby. I was just Goldie. *Fuck, Goldie* was what he would utter once in a blue moon, but he remained silent for the most part.

Imagine how angry I fucking felt hearing him call this little bitch BABY! I saw red, and the same hate I felt for her, I started to feel for him, because he was instigating everything and should have never fucked her. I remember looking down into her hand and seeing that she still had the knife in it as she continued to push toward me. I reached around Grim, grabbed her hand that held the knife, and pulled it toward his stomach.

I popped my eyes open and looked at Grim laid out in the passenger seat. He made me do that by picking her over me, and I had no choice, but as long as he believed it was Kaliyah and she thought the same, I could worm my way back by his side. Hopefully, this time, he wouldn't cross me! I could overlook the fact that he fucked that bitch and kissed her. I still didn't understand how she came to know the damn code for his phone like that, but I could look past that… as long as he acted right this time.

I looked at him, and I did love him more than anything. He was worth giving a second chance to.

"She did this, Optimus. I had no reason to do this to him. I love him," I finally spoke up.

"Yeah? Tell me… did you love him when you were sitting on my dick last night?" he asked, and I flicked my eyes up at him. He had a mean mug on his face, and I rolled my eyes. I knew fucking him was a huge mistake!

Twenty minutes later, we pulled up to the hospital. Goliath got out and picked up Grim. Optimus rushed into the hospital and yelled out for some help.

I trailed behind Goliath, staring at Grim's lifeless body. None of this would have happened if he had just chosen me. Did I want to kill him? At the time, yes… I did, because I knew at that point that she was who he wanted and not me. Yes, I wanted him to die. Now, I could see that everything had hopefully worked in my favor.

Kaliyah believed she stabbed him, and so did he, from the way he called out her name once it happened. I knew she wouldn't dare show her face here, leaving me free to be there for Grim.

Once he saw how I held him down, he wouldn't be able to deny that he loves me. Smiling to myself, I said a little prayer that he would make it and followed him into the hospital. When he was placed on a stretcher, I gave him a sensual kiss on the lips. Both Optimus and Goliath looked at me, but they could go and fuck themselves for all I care!

Sucking his teeth and chuckling, Optimus pushed me aside to whisper some things into Grim's ear. The doctors then rushed him down the hall and into surgery. I turned to head for the waiting area, but Optimus grabbed my arm and roughly pulled me into his body.

"As long as I live, my nigga will never wife a thot like you. I fucked you because I could… not because I wanted you. If Grim wanted your ass, he would have never told me that I could," he snarled in my ear before releasing me. My eyes bucked at what he just revealed to me. I started fucking with Optimus, hoping it would make Grim jealous and tell me to stop, but I had no fucking idea that the whole time, he had told Optimus that he could step to me! Like I was a pair of sneakers that he no longer wanted, Grim had passed me to the next nigga. I looked down the hall where they just wheeled Grim down and I wished that he did die!

Chapter Three

Kaliyah Diamond

I WOKE UP TO FIND THAT I was sitting in darkness in the same spot I was in when I was holding Deshaun. His blood was still on my hands and all over my pajamas. I could smell it and feel the stickiness of it. Someone must have turned the lights out without me noticing, because they were on before.

I rose to my feet and walked over to turn them on. I cringed at the sight of Deshaun's blood in a puddle, staining the cream plush carpet. I opened my bedroom door, and the rest of the house was quiet. I was conflicted. I didn't know whether to try and go to the hospital to see if I killed him or not. I wanted to know, but I didn't at the same time. It would absolutely crush me to know that I killed him after everything he had done for me and the fact that I did love him, but I was also afraid. I knew that if he had survived, he was going to kill me anyway.

I had heard stories from Pedra about how he killed people that did any kind of harm to him, and although I wasn't trying to hurt him, I did! My mind was spinning. I didn't know what to do. Did I stay here and wait until he came back home to kill me, or did I run while I still could?

Plus, there was still the fact that Goldie could come back anytime too and finish what she had started. I knew I didn't have the strength to fight with her for a second time. I rubbed my hands over my face and paced the bedroom floor as I thought. I didn't really have many places to go, and I didn't know the area like that. I knew enough… like my grandmother's house, my school, the grocery store, and other places like the park or mall, but I didn't know outside of that.

I didn't have friends, so I had never needed to go anywhere or visit other areas like that. I lived a sheltered life, spending most of my teen years hiding.

"Why is my life like this? Why can't I just catch a break? Was this all I was destined for... pain, misery, and problems?" I yelled out in the quiet room. I shook my head and sighed. I was tired... beyond tired. I was tired of running and fighting for my life... tired of hurting and crying. I knew I was the cause of Deshaun getting hurt and why I may need to go on the run again, but it would have never happened if Goldie had never come into my room trying to attack me first.

My eyes fell to the puddle of Deshaun's blood, and I closed them. *God... at least spare his life, if nothing else,* I silently prayed. I don't know why I did, because it was obvious my prayers were never heard. I prayed for my mother more times than I could remember, and our relationship only got worse.

Suddenly, I thought of something, and it sent a chill down my spine. If I had killed Deshaun, Optimus would kill me anyway. I saw the way he looked at me, and I didn't like it. Goldie told Optimus how I just stabbed Deshaun for no reason, and by his facial expression, I think he believed it. I couldn't even call Pedra for help, because Optimus was her cousin, and he would easily find me.

I started panicking as I imagined that he was on his way to get me. Once again, I had to run away. I rushed around my room and started filling my backpack. Deshaun had bought me a few clothes since being here, but I didn't take those. I thought it would have been wrong for me to do so.

There was one thing that I could be thankful for and that was that this time. I had money since I had been working, and at least I wouldn't be left finding

somewhere outside to sleep. Once I gathered everything I needed, I changed out of my bloody clothes, throwing on a T-shirt and tights. I slipped my feet in my sneakers and grabbed my bag. I knew that the house was empty, but I still cautiously opened the bedroom door and looked around before I stepped out.

My breathing became heavy and quickened as I tiptoed through the dark house toward the front door. I was panicking so much that I could barely breathe. I was afraid of being caught before I could leave, and I was afraid to go out there again alone. Deshaun didn't know what would happen between us since we made love last night, but he assured me that whatever would happen, we would do it together. Now, I had lost that, and I was alone.

When I pulled the front door open and the cool early hour morning air hit my face, tears fell from my eyes, because I knew at that point that I would never see Deshaun again. As I closed the door behind me, I felt my heart break in two.

Chapter Four

Deborah 'Tuts' Diamond

TODAY WAS MY MAMA'S FUNERAL. She drove me crazy and stayed trying to tell me what to do, even though my ass was grown at thirty-nine, but I didn't want her to die. I was hurt and angry when I found out, especially because my own fucking daughter caused it.

It was from her fucking selfish actions that my mama got sick. She always had a weak heart, but Kaliyah pushed her beyond that point, and she suffered a heart attack. The little bitch didn't even come home to see if I was okay. I didn't know where the hell she was, but if I ever found out, I would beat her ass! She caused all this mayhem in my life, and when she was satisfied, she left me to deal with it all alone... and I was selfish?

I was trying to help us! We needed money, and all she had to do was open her fucking legs, take a little dick, and we would have been able to eat like royalty. How hard was that? It wasn't like Silvan was an ugly nigga. I would have fucked him myself, given the chance, but the nigga didn't want me. He wanted her. The bitch was lucky, and that still wasn't good enough for her. It was okay for me to sell myself to keep her clothed throughout the years, but she was too good to do it?

Yeah, I was better off without her, and I still don't think my brother raped her. I think she fucked him, and that's why he was in my face, protecting her. I knew there was a reason why he was up in my business like that.

He had to spend three days in the hospital after that nigga broke in and beat our asses. I woke up, and my whole body felt like it was on fire from that ass whooping. I didn't even know who the fuck he was or how he even got into my house to begin with, but I knew it was something to do with Kaliyah. Silvan probably had enough of me telling him I didn't know where she was, so he must have sent them to teach me a lesson. I should have put out a missing persons' report for her, but honestly… I didn't do it, because I knew once I found her, I was going to beat her ass unconscious and see how she liked it. I didn't need any fucking police in my life that would prevent me from doing that.

I don't know what was up with Simeon, but since he came home, he locked himself in his room, and I had not seen him or heard anything from him since. I hope he wasn't dead in there, because that nigga still owed me money for fucking my damn daughter, and I wanted that shit… especially as Silvan was no longer accepting my calls.

Kaliyah wasn't here, and she was still fucking up my life! Silvan was the only one that was allowing me to get my shit without payment, because I promised that he could have that little bitch once I did find her. She was no longer welcomed in my home, and whatever he wanted to do with her was not my business. At first, he wasn't into it, but I promised him he could have her instead of just coming to the house to fuck her, and surprisingly, he agreed, but it had been weeks since I had heard from him.

Nobody around had seen him. His absence was forcing me to go without my stuff when I didn't have any money, and it was killing me. I had to sell things in my house and Kaliyah's clothes to get some money. Why did my fucking daughter hate me so much and make my life a living hell?

The funeral was due to start in an hour. My mama left money to pay for it which was good, because I didn't have a dime spare to put toward it. I must say I was angry to know that she didn't leave any money for me! She left her apartment to both Simeon and me, but my ass couldn't do shit with it without his say so. Even in the grave, she was letting my brother control me. She had set up a college fund for Zoe and Kaliyah. Too bad both of those bitches were too stupid for college.

I smoothed down the black bodycon dress that I had on and outed my cigarette. I stood to my feet and headed for my brother's room. If I had to go to this funeral, then so did he!

"SIMEON!!"

I pounded on his door with my fist.

"Open this door!" I hollered and kicked it. Seconds later, I heard him unlocking the door. When he opened it and I took a look at him, for the first time, I felt a little bad for my brother. He looked scruffy, his beard was all gray and untidy, his hair was in desperate need of a trim, and his clothes were all wrinkled. His eyes were red and puffy, making him look like he hadn't slept in weeks. He no longer looked like my brother, and I was sorry that I had to get him like that to begin with.

However, I wasn't all to blame. Kaliyah caused him to be here. Plus, he needed to take some of the blame too. When I offered for him to leave, he should have taken it!

"What do you want, Deborah?" he asked in a soft voice.

"Mama's funeral starts in an hour, Simeon, and you're not even ready." I tapped my foot at him and folded my arms across my chest.

"It's Wednesday today?" he asked, and I nodded my head yes.

"Oh… I'ma get ready then," he said, looking bewildered as he scratched his head.

"Simeon, do you have any money?" I asked just as he turned around. He slowly looked back at me, and his eyes darkened.

"I'm not giving you any money to get any more of that shit!" he suddenly barked at me.

"Don't worry what I use the money for! That's my business, not yours!

Besides, you owe me money, nigga!" I yelled back.

"For what? I don't owe you shit."

"Yes, the fuck you do! You owe me money for fucking my daughter!" I yelled, and his eyes bucked out of his head. I had never ever mentioned that Kaliyah told me what happened until now, so I knew he was shocked to hear what I just said.

"You two were fucking around and cost me money, so you better pay me for it," I said with a hand out. He dropped his head and slumped his shoulders.

"You have some serious problems, Debbie, and you need help," he said with his eyes still down, looking at the floor.

"I need help? You were having sex with your own niece!"

I snorted and shook my head. Here this nigga was… a pot calling a kettle black.

"SHE DIDN'T HAVE SEX WITH ME!" he suddenly erupted, and I stepped back. His eyes flashed black as he stared at me.

"She didn't."

He shook his head and mumbled something under his breath.

"You already know what I did, because she would have never told you that we had sex," he lifted his head and said.

"Don't you care where she is, Debbie? Are you not worried? She's been gone for almost two months."

"Because of what you did!"

"I KNOW WHAT I DID!" he yelled, making his voice bounce off of my walls. "And don't you think I feel fucked up about it? Every fucking day… I wish I would just die knowing what the fuck I did, but I know what you did!" he yelled, making his voice bounce off of my walls. He pointed at me and stepped toward me, making me back up to the wall.

"You fed me fucking drugs, and I know you did! I've never even smoked a cigarette a day in my life, so there was no fucking reason for me to have fucking coke in my system! I swear to God, Debbie, you're one fucked up person and so ugly inside. If you weren't my sister, I would have beaten your fucking ass by now!" he said, backing away from me and turning around to close his door.

"But that's not why you won't hit me, Simeon… is it?" I asked, and he stopped in his tracks.

"You won't hit me because you feel guilty," I pushed, and he swung around to face me.

"Shut up, Debbie," he told me, pointing a finger at me.

"Admit it. That's the real reason why you haven't beaten my ass yet… isn't it?" I continued.
"Debbie, shut the fuck up!"

"No, admit it!"

I walked up to him and pushed him back hard.

"Admit that you won't beat my ass because you feel guilty

from not saving me from daddy!" I cried out, and he shut his eyes tightly.

"I told you daddy was touching me, and you refused to listen to me. You never believed me until I got pregnant with Zoe! I was your baby sister, and you failed me! In the end, I had to give birth to my own father's child, and that's the real reason why you took Zoe away from me… because of your guilt!" I yelled at him, and he grabbed me.

"AND I KILLED HIM FOR YOU!!!" he screamed in my face.

This family was beyond fucked up. My daughter should have been my sister. My brother raped his own niece, and my daughter had sex with her sister! The sad part of it all was my mama died not knowing any of this. Simeon killed our dad after Zoe was born, and he finally knew what I had been telling him was true. I told my mama it was a random guy who I got pregnant by, and she was told that our dad was killed during a mugging. If only she knew, but thanks to Kaliyah, she died before I could tell her the truth. Man, I hated my daughter!

Chapter Five

Simeon

L IFE WASN'T ALWAYS THIS FUCKED UP. Debbie and I had a good life as kids. Our parents had separated when Debbie was born, but our pops stayed an active part in our lives. In fact, we lived with him from Thursdays to Sundays and spent the rest of the time with our mother. In an ideal world, our parents would have been together, and maybe half of the shit that happened wouldn't have, but it worked at the time.

Everything was going good. Our pops was a hardworking man and damn good father to us. He made sure that we never needed for anything. He and my mama worked around the schedule when they had us, and both had really good jobs. I thought life was sweet until Debbie started telling me that our dad was touching her. She was twelve at the time, and I was twenty-two.

I heard what she was telling me, but I refused to believe that shit. My Dad, Bryant, was the epitome of a man and everything that I was striving to be like. There was just no way that he could be doing what she said that he was. I brushed it off and decided that maybe she misunderstood what was taking place during her bath time.

My pops was the kind of dad who would physically put our little asses in the bath tub and scrub us from head to toe. He didn't play that going back to our mama dirty and shit. He would make damn sure that we were washing ourselves properly. Debbie was a girl, and I knew that vaginas were different from dicks with all the folds and shit it had. I knew that when my pops cleaned her downstairs, she took it as something else.

When I witnessed him bathing her one night, and I saw how he quickly washed between her legs with his eyes closed, I knew it was nothing like she was telling me, and I waved it off. I even told her not to go around and say that shit out loud before people believed it was how she was trying to make it seem.

Shit went back to normal after that for the most part, and although sometimes Debbie tried to bring that shit up a few times, it was not like before where she was complaining almost daily. I knew she was just taking things the wrong way.

I was adamant that I was right until the dreadful day my mama called me crying to say that Debbie was pregnant at the age of fourteen! I was twenty-four at that point, and I admit that I spent less and less time at home, because I had a girl and a job which took up most of my time. It killed me to know that I was so busy that I failed to keep an eye on my baby sister and that she got pregnant as a result of it.

My anger got the best of me, and I almost beat Debbie's ass. She had people out here talking about my family and how my fast ass sister got pregnant at such a young age. That shit ate me up, and when I confronted her to find out who the fuck the father was, she blew me away by telling me it was our own dad! How was I supposed to process that shit?

Of course, the love I had for my pops caused me to accuse my sister of terrible things, and it wasn't until I physically yoked her up that she told me the father was some young nigga named Micah.

When I took my ass down to his house, I couldn't believe that I was looking at some not about shit little nigga who was only fucking fifteen years old! Debbie admitted to fucking him one time, and for me, that was one time too many. I beat that little nigga's ass for laying a hand on my got damn sister.

She kept her pregnancy hidden from us, and by the time my mama found out, she was six months, and it was too late to do shit about it.

After Zoe was born, something inside of me was telling me that Debbie was telling the truth. Zoe looked like Debbie did when she was born, but I noticed that she had features of my dad that not even Debbie had. All it took was one look at her, and I knew. I knew in my heart that that sick son of a bitch had been touching on my sister this whole time.

I didn't tell anyone what I was doing. After Debbie tried to tell me it was our dad that first time, she never said it again, but I couldn't let it go. I had the baby and did a DNA test after taking one of my pop's toothbrushes. When the results came back, I almost died.

How could my pops, the man who helped bring me and my sister here, lay with his own daughter and create a child? My mind couldn't comprehend that; however, it couldn't deny that the truth was out. I know you must be wondering if I confronted that sick bastard, and I sure as hell fucking did! At first, he tried to deny it until I showed him that I had proof that he had fathered Zoe...

"That is what the fuck your mama gets!" he yelled at me when he finally figured out that I knew the truth.

"What the fuck are you talking about? How the hell is this my mama's fault... because she didn't want your perverted ass?"

I ran up on him with my fists clenched tight.

*"Because she made me believe that Debbie was my fucking
daughter, and I know she's not!"*

*I had no idea if what he was saying was the truth or not,
but I failed to see what the fuck that had to do with Debbie!*

*"Nigga, you should have gone to my mama about that, not
fuck my little sister and get her ass pregnant!"*

He glared at me and laughed an evil laugh.

*"This was much more fun, and damn did I enjoy that shit,"
he said.*

Those words that came out of his mouth haunted to this day! I
should have reported his ass to the police. It's just that I believed
jail would be too good for that nigga, and he didn't deserve to live
after that.

The next night, I followed him from his apartment, and after
watching that nasty nigga fuck a young looking prostitute, I made
my move. He had climbed out to dispose of the condom he used,
and I climbed in from the back- passenger side. When he got back
in the car, I moved and held a gun to the back of his head. He had
parked his car on an abandoned road underneath a train station, so
I wasn't worried about being seen.

The nigga didn't even beg for his life. Instead, he laughed at
me and called me out on failing to protect my sister. When he told
me that I was just like him, and sooner or later, that side would
come out, I lost my temper and shot him. I didn't even flinch or
care that I had killed him. I just got out of the car and left him
there. The police found him the next day, and they suspected that he
was maybe killed by a prostitute or fiend from where his body
was discovered, and the case was closed.

After that, I couldn't live with my failure to protect Debbie and decided to move away to Boston to start over but not without Zoe. Sometime between her giving birth to Zoe and me killing our dad, Debbie had changed. She was staying out all night, fucking random men in our mama's house, and not caring for Zoe. I knew she was acting out because of what happened to her, and I felt responsible. I tried to help her, but I couldn't stick around due to guilt I felt.

I believed that I was doing the best for Debbie at the time, because I knew it wouldn't have been easy to see Zoe's face, knowing who her father was. Though my mama never knew what my pops had done, she agreed that Zoe would have been better off with me. We both thought that Debbie would definitely straighten out, however, her behavior worsened to the point where I completely left her alone.

A part of me wanted to deal with her and make her straighten. The other part couldn't get over the fact that I had let her down, and it was that part I followed. I stayed away from Debbie.

A few years later, she got pregnant with Kaliyah. I was scared, thinking that history would have repeated itself. However, Debbie surprised us. She was a good mom to Kaliyah. I started visiting again, and it was like she was my Debbie again. We were able to laugh and talk like the old days. She was no longer haunted by the things my pops had done to her, and her life was on track.

She was still messing with random niggas, but she wasn't smoking weed anymore and hanging out all night. We continued to have a good relationship until she stopped coming around me and answering my calls when Kaliyah turned twelve. Even my mama, who only lived less than twenty minutes away from her, wasn't seeing them often. Even Kaliyah had changed. She wasn't that bubbly, happy, and outspoken child that she used to be. She was quiet and never really spoke to anyone. I didn't want to think the worst about my sister, but the signs were all there.

Like before, I chose to hide and ignore them. I hid and acted like everything was okay… That was until my mama called me that night to tell me how Debbie was trying to sell Kaliyah for drugs. Just as she was on a right path, Debbie slipped, but this time worse than before. She was no longer smoking weed, because she was on something much stronger.

That night I arrived at her door, that inner guilty Simeon told me not to go, but I knew I was only making my sister worse! I should have stepped in from before and did what I was supposed to do instead of running away. At that point, I made a choice that I was going to stick around, no matter what. I couldn't let Kaliyah suffer for the mistakes I had made. All of this could have been avoided if I had listened to my baby sister when she first came to me and told me what our pops was doing to her.

As you can imagine, Debbie wasn't very happy with the idea of me being around, but I knew what was best for her, and I was doing it for her own good… that was until all kinds of thoughts and visions began seeping into my head. I should have known at that point that something wasn't right with me, but then that would be me having to come to terms that my own sister was feeding me drugs, and I just didn't want to believe it.

If only I had listened to my gut that was telling me I was getting sick, none of this would be happening. My niece wouldn't have been missing, and I wouldn't have done the most unthinkable thing a man could ever do to a family member. I was supposed to protect her. Instead, I became the very man I was supposed to protect her from! God knows that I was sick!

I saw my niece, but I never *saw* her… if that makes sense. It was like she was a stranger to me. Drugs effect everybody in different ways, and for some reason, it made me horny… but not your average *let's make love* horny. It was like a rage… an animalistic feeling that I couldn't control. Feelings of pain and death flashed through my bones, and I fed into those feelings and hurt my baby niece.

I felt nothing after, and I didn't until I woke up in the hospital. When that nigga whooped my ass, I thought I was going to die. I had never felt pain like I did that night. Even after they had left and Debbie woke me up, my body felt like my soul was leaving me. The demons started when I woke up and tried going cold turkey. I literally woke up in cold sweats and tears running down my face as the revelation of what I had done haunted me.

I knew she wouldn't want to see me, but when I was released, I looked for Kaliyah. I searched everywhere and asked anyone who would stop for me if they had seen her, but it was like she had disappeared. That both made me happy and scared, because I knew she was somewhere that neither me or her mama could hurt her again, but I had no idea if she was safe or, God forbid, dead somewhere.

It pained me that Debbie did nothing and didn't even try to find her. I couldn't tell her what I did, not that I was trying to hide it, but the words were just too painful to even form in my mouth. *I HAD RAPED MY OWN NIECE!*

How do those type of words come freely out of a person's mouth? However, I knew sooner or later I would have to tell my sister what I had done, and I was somewhat relieved when she brought it up. She made me angry by insinuating that it was consensual incest sex, especially as I knew Kaliyah would never tell her something like that. At least she knew without me having to tell her.

I was hurt when she actually asked for money, and at that point, I knew my sister was well and truly gone. There was no way my daughter could ever come to me and tell me what my brother did to her, and all I would do about it was ask him for some money! My sister was lost, and I needed to come to terms with it.

***

At my mama's funeral, I sat alone, way in the back with my head down and shades on. I missed my mama, but I knew I helped with her death. What no one knew was that I told my mother what I had done to Kaliyah...

"Simy, where is my grandbaby? I don't understand what you mean that she is missing! How and why? This is why I asked you to come... so something like this wouldn't happen!"

My mama paced her living room. I had just been released from the hospital, and I went to go and see her. Debbie was in the streets as usual... acting like things were okay while Kaliyah was out there somewhere alone!

"Mama, please calm down. You know you have a weak heart!" I pleaded, but that fell on deaf ears. I could see her breathing quickening, and I was afraid for her. She always had problems with her heart and anxiety. The last thing I wanted was something to happen to her on top of everything else.

"Simy, we need to look for her! What if that terrible man has her?" she asked, mirroring my fear. I knew Debbie had been

trying to get that tall light skinned nigga into the house to fuck with Kaliyah, but after I threatened his life and hers, he never came back to the house. Now that Kaliyah was out of the house, who knew if he had finally caught up with her, and if he did, that would have been on me.

"Mama, I need to tell you something," I said looking at her. I didn't want to have to tell her, but my guilt was eating me up daily, and I couldn't take it anymore.

"What, baby? What do you need to tell me?"

She rubbed my cheek, and I took her hand. I didn't deserve her affection. Choking on the tears that were now flowing, I responded.

"I did something very bad mama... something so terrible, and that's why Kaliyah is gone."

She looked at me and tried to wipe my tears, but I stopped her. I didn't even give her a chance to ask me anymore questions before I blurted it out.

"I raped her, mama! I raped Kaliyah!"

As soon as the words left my mouth, she jumped to her feet and slapped me across the face.

"Simeon, you did not do that! Tell me you didn't do no nasty, crazy, and sick thing like that to my baby!"

"Mama, I didn't mean it! I was strung out on drugs, and I did it. I wasn't myself, mama!"

She backed up from me, and I grabbed her.

"Please, mama. Don't do that. You know I wouldn't do anything like that if I wasn't sick," I begged her on my knees.

"I sent you here to help Kaliyah, not help yourself to her! What the hell were you doing on that mess anyway?"

She slapped me again. I knew I should have told her what Deborah had done, but I just couldn't. I continued hanging on to my mama, begging for her forgiveness. It was almost like my soul opened, and I couldn't stop my confession. The fact I killed my pops fell out of my mouth before I could stop it, and the reason why followed. My mama stopped moving, trying to push me off of her, and when I looked up at her, it was like she was struggling to breathe.

"MAMA!"

I jumped to my feet and screamed. Her eyes bulged out of her head, and I could see that she was gasping for air. Then, she fell to the ground and closed her eyes. I did everything in my power to get her breathing again, and when the paramedics came, they took over for me. I guess the pain I unleashed was too much, because my mama never recovered, and she died the next morning.

Tears slid down my face as I sat thinking about all that I did. My life and the lives of my family were in turmoil, and if I could have gone back in time to fix it all, I would.

As of now, my niece was still missing, and my mama was dead. I was losing the will to live, but I still needed to make something right before I left this earth which could be sooner than later.

"Bye, mama. Please forgive me," I whispered to myself where I sat. I felt too ashamed to go to the front and see her, so I quietly left. There was some place I needed to go!

Deshaun 'Grim' Jones

"*BITCHES ARE NOT WORTH IT, SON! Don't ever fall in love. Do you hear me? No matter what you do for them, it will never ever be enough. Even if you kill another nigga for them, it's not enough! I wished I never loved yo' mama, but I do. Where I was weak, you will be strong, Deshaun. Don't ever love a bitch!*"

I remembered being twelve years old and having that conversation with my pops, wondering what the hell he was talking about. I don't know why I was remembering this, but as my mind drifted between what was real and what wasn't, it played like a movie. I knew I wasn't dead, because I could hear everything, but I couldn't open my eyes.

I willed my body to wake up, but it wouldn't. Instead, it had me trapped in a void in my mind where my life flashed. My pops groomed me and raised me up to never fall in love, and so I didn't until I met Kaliyah. She was unlike anybody I had ever come across, and God knows I didn't want to love her, but I did.

I pray she's okay, Lord... please, I thought and hoped. I didn't know where I was or how long I had been here, but I knew it was nowhere near her. I couldn't hear her voice or smell her scent. Why wouldn't my body wake up? I needed to find her and make sure she was okay. I knew she never meant to hurt me. Goldie caused this!

I had heard the commotion coming from Kaliyah's room, and God... my heart was beating out of my chest as I ran to her room. She was putting up a fight against Goldie, and I should have protected her. I should have put Goldie out that night. I had been seeing the way she would look at Kaliyah whenever she saw her, and I hated it. I promised to protect Kaliyah from the night I found her in the abandoned building, and I had failed.

Goldie fucked up her face, and my heart broke when I saw her bruised eye. All her life she had to fight her family, and I brought her into another situation where she had to fight.

I felt my leg suddenly twitch, and my eyes rolled in their sockets. I don't care what I needed to do, but I was going to get my ass up and find my girl. Goldie better hope she hadn't touched another hair on her fucking head. *Get the fuck up Grim, you pussy,* I cursed at myself. Being out like this was not a fucking option. I needed to find Kaliyah. *Lord, if you can hear… please wake me up!*

Chapter Six

Kaliyah Diamond

YESTERDAY WAS MY GRANDMOTHER'S FUNERAL, and it killed me that I couldn't even go to it. Zoe had emailed me to let me know, and I wished that I could have gone, but I was too afraid that I would see my mother or even my uncle. I never wanted to see them again, to be honest. This was my second day in the hotel, and I was driving myself crazy. I still didn't know if Deshaun was okay or not, but I decided that enough was enough. I needed to find out.

I pulled on an oversized gray hoodie with black jeans and Adidas sneakers. I put on a cap and big shades that swallowed up my small face. I was trying to hide as much of my face as I could, just in case somebody recognized me. I was about to go down to the hospital just to find out if he was okay.

My heart was beating as I climbed out of the Uber that I had taken to the hospital. I looked around again and pulled my cap down lower. I dropped my head as I casually and slowly walked into the hospital.

I went to the front desk and asked for Deshaun Jones. I wasn't expecting to have to hand over my ID before she would tell me, and I just hoped that information was confidential, because I didn't want anyone to know that I came. After finding out where he was, I made my way to his room. When I found it, I stood frozen in the same spot. The nurse never said whether he was awake or not, and that frightened me.

"Excuse me. Can I help you?" a voice came from behind me saying, making me jump out of my skin.

"Um… no. I was just looking for the restroom," I said as she looked me over.

"It's just over there, sweetie."

She smiled at me. She was a nice looking lady with braids and a caramel complexion. She was a little taller than me and looked to be about thirty years old.

"Thank you."

I smiled and looked back at the door to Deshaun's room just to make sure no one had come out of it.

"Do you know someone in that room?" the nurse asked me.

"No, but I was here when he was brought in. I was just wondering how he was," I said, and she looked at me.

"I'm sorry. I can't give you that kind of information," she said, and I nodded. After a few seconds of silence, she spoke up again.

"Who were you visiting at the time when you saw him being brought in?"

I couldn't even answer her because as soon as I gave a name, she would know that I was lying. She stepped closer to me, and at that point, I knew she was about to call security on me or something.

"You never heard this from me. He's out of surgery and is stable, but he won't be awaking for another few hours at least. The doctor gave him something to make him comfortable," she whispered, winking at me.

"Thank you."

I smiled, and she nodded her head before walking away. I was saddened to know that he needed surgery because of what I had done to him, but I was relieved that he made it out okay. It's a shame that I would probably never get to see him again because of what happened. I would do anything to go back to that night and not pick up the knife, because I lost the one good thing that had ever happened to me.

I stood and watched his door for a few more seconds, before wiping the tears that were sliding down my face and leaving the hospital never to return again.

***

I decided after leaving the hospital that I would go and visit my grandmother. I needed to at least see her. I needed to make peace with the fact that I wasn't there and that she died because of me.

I was shown to her graveside, and as soon as I saw it, I broke down. I knew she had died, but seeing it made it all too real. I couldn't get over the guilt I felt for running away. I never ever thought my grandmother would have taken ill as a result, and I regretted not going to her and telling her what was happening.

"Grandma, I'm so sorry."

I sniveled and sat on my knees in front of her grave. Imagining the pain, she must have gone through and how she must have suffered made me cry even harder. I thought I was protecting her by running away, because I couldn't bring myself to tell her what her children were doing. I thought it was better if she never knew, and in the end, it caused her more pain.

"I should have told you. I should have come to you, but I was afraid," I blubbered like a baby. I removed my shades so that I could wipe my eyes. I sat on the ground, drifting in and out of different thoughts.

I wondered what would have happened if I had gone to my grandmother and tell her what was going on. Would she have made me go to the police? Would I have been forced to go back home to them? Would my uncle have abused me again? Would Silvan have succeeded? I knew my grandmother loved me, but what could she have done, and how could she have stopped it?

My grandmother sadly died for my actions, and one day, I would be able to forgive myself for that, but I stood by my decision to leave. I don't know what would have happened to me, and I could think about all the *what ifs,* but my gut was telling me it would have only been worse if I stayed. Smiling through my tears, I remembered the good times with my grandma that I would forever cherish.

"Goodbye, Grandma... sleep in peace. I love you and always will. I hope you forgive me," I said, standing to my feet. I pushed my shades back on and turned around to leave. When I did, I was standing face to face with my uncle! I tried to run, but he grabbed me.

"I'm sorry, baby girl. I'm so sorry!" he yelled, dropping to his knees while still holding me.

"Don't call me that! Don't ever call me that again!"

I pushed him and tried to squirm out of his hold, but he just held on tighter.

I looked around, hoping someone was around to help me, but I was all alone. "Kaliyah, listen to me!"

"No!" I screamed.

"I'm sorry. I was messed up, Kaliyah. Your mama fed me drugs. I saw your face, but I never saw *you*, Kaliyah. It was like I didn't know who you were. You know if I wasn't strung out like that, I would have never hurt you," he said, and I stopped struggling. I knew he was on drugs. It was plain to see from his eyes, but I never knew it was my mama who gave them to him.

"She had been putting drugs into my food, and I got so high. I lost my senses, and I di—" he started, but his voice croaked. I looked into his eyes, and I could see his tears that he didn't even attempt to wipe away. At that point, I knew he never intended on hurting me. It never changed the fact that it still happened, but I felt some type of relief to know that he was not himself when he did it.

"I've not been able to sleep since I realized what I did. Someone broke into the house and beat us up. When I woke up, I was in the hospital. I started going through withdrawals, and what I did started haunting me. I looked for you, and I'm sorry that your mother didn't," he said, wiping his cheek.

"I know that sorry cannot undo what I did, and I don't expect you to forgive me. I just need you to know that I'm sorry, Kaliyah. God knows that I'm sorry, and if I could go back to that day and not do it, I would," he said, and I nodded.

"Looking at you now, I can see that you've been well and looking after yourself. So, I'm going to tell you this… do not ever go back home, Kaliyah."

I was never planning on going back there, ever. He didn't need to tell me that, but I was shocked to hear him telling me not to.

"Stay away from your mama, Kaliyah. She's not right, and she will only end up hurting you. Be strong, Kaliyah, and look after yourself. No matter what, nana loved you so much, and her death was not your fault. It was mine and your mama's for the things we did to you. I'm going away now. I just came to tell my mama bye. I'm going to give myself up to the police. Don't worry. You won't need to go to court or anything. I explained everything to a detective, and they took forensics from our rooms. They found the underwear I destroyed and your blood in my room amongst some other things... plus, the 'friend' I was with at the time reported it as well," he said, and my eyes opened widely in shock.

"I have until the end of the day to hand myself over," he said, giving me a weak smile.

"Take care, baby girl. At least now I can do my bid in peace knowing that I saw you."

He tapped my shoulder, kissed a flower, and placed it on top of my grandmother's grave before I walked away.

I always wondered how I would feel if I ever saw my uncle again, which is why I didn't go to the funeral yesterday, but I admit, it was a bittersweet moment. I felt torn, because he hurt me beyond words. I felt like it would forever haunt me, but at the same time, I felt sorry for him.

My mama was evil to hook her own brother on that mess, and I knew for a fact that it was to make him numb enough for her to do what she wanted without his control. I just prayed that my uncle would be able to pick up his life again after this and as for my mother... what mother?

Chapter Seven

Goldie Lawson

GRIM'S SURGERY WAS SUCCESSFUL, and he had been out of surgery for a few days. The knife ripped his spleen and caused him to bleed out. He lost a lot of blood and needed a transfusion on top of the surgery to repair the damage. Doctors said that he should make a full recovery and that the wound wasn't fatal... lucky for him!

I was currently sitting in the hospital chair which was opposite Grim's bed. As I sat here picking at and filing my nails, I couldn't keep myself from mean mugging Grim as he was sleeping in his bed. This nigga broke my heart and played me to the fucking left like I was nothing. SIX YEARS, and he passed me to the next nigga!

Why was I still here? I wish I knew. Despite all of that... despite Optimus telling me how Grim told him to make his move on me, I still loved that no good son of a bitch. I was hopeful after a near death experience that he would get his shit together and wife me. I couldn't give a fuck what Optimus or any of his stupid ass niggas had to say about the situation. Grim was no angel either! Everybody makes mistakes, and I wasn't going to let anybody get in the way of what I wanted. Grim and I were destined to be together. I left my boyfriend of three years for this nigga! He at least owed me that.

I looked up at him and rolled my eyes. I don't know if it was possible to love someone as much as you hated them, but that's how I felt about Grim at this moment. I watched as his eyes rolled around in their sockets, something that he'd been doing for the last hour.

"What?" I said and sat up in my seat when I saw his leg twitch. That was something he hadn't done before. I slowly stood to my feet and walked over to him. If I wanted to kill him now as he slept, I could, but everybody would know that it was me. His parents had the nurses make everybody sign in and out of the room, so they would know that I was the last person to have been in here... lucky for him!

I looked down at his face, and my heart skipped a beat. He was just so handsome, so sweet, and I felt my heart swell with all the love I had for him. I stroked his face gently before running a finger along his beautifully thick and sexy lips. That night we brought him into the hospital was the first time my lips had ever touched his, and it felt like heaven. I remembered seeing how comfortable Kaliyah looked kissing him, leading me to believe that he had *been* kissing her.

"Why do you keep on hurting me, Grim?" I whispered more to myself than him. What could he really see and want in a young girl like that? She didn't have anything to offer him like I did. My body was perfection. Niggas always told me how good I felt and how beautiful my body was. They just couldn't get enough of me... even Optimus' hating ass. That nigga stayed calling my got damn phone, pressing me for some pussy. Everybody and their pops wanted me, so why didn't Grim?

I looked down at his face again and sighed. He was killing me, but I couldn't stop loving him.

"Um, who the hell are you?" I heard behind me and swung around to see a beautiful older woman looking at me. Before I could even respond to her, the door opened again, and a giant man walked through the door. His head almost touched the top of the doorway from how tall he was. Immediately, I could tell that he was Grim's father, because they looked exactly the same. I knew of his parent's, but I had never met them before.

"Well?" the woman said, because I had yet

to respond to her. "I'm Goldie… I'm—"

"Oh, you're Goldie?"

His pop's deep voice shook my ear drums. I smiled and looked down at Grim. He was constantly playing games, trying to convince me that he didn't care about me, but his dad just showed me that was a lie. If he never cared for me, he never would have told his dad about me.

"You know this girl?" Grim's mother asked.

"Yeah, he told me he fucks with her sometimes," his dad said, and my smile dropped.

"Oh, Goldie… the lady he has staying at his house?" she asked, and his dad nodded.

"Oh, isn't she with Optimus now?" his mother added, and I looked back down at Grim. I was the bitch he was fucking with that stayed in his house and was now with his best friend… not the girl that he's been seeing for years? Why the fuck did I have to be *staying with him*? Why couldn't we be living together? Why the fuck would he tell them that I was with Optimus? *I hate this nigga,* I thought as I looked at him. He wasn't going to disrespect me anymore!

I saw from the corner of my eyes that his mother approached his bed. I turned to look at her, and she looked at me like I had no right to be close to her son.

"Excuse me," she said, even though I could tell from her tone that she didn't want to ask. I stepped aside so that she could approach her son. She stroked his face and kissed him on his forehead. I turned to see his dad looking at me with a smirk on his face. He knew his comment made me feel some type of way, and he didn't care.

All kinds of murderous thoughts flowed through my mind like an overflowing river. Grim made me look stupid in front of his parents... something that he would die regretting. I smiled at his dad and flicked my hair off my shoulders. Let's see how happy he was going to look when his son was dead! I was not about to let this one go.

I turned toward the chair that I had been sitting in and picked up my purse.

"I will leave you two alone with your son," I said quietly and headed to the door. Pulling it open I made a vow that this was the last day I allowed Grim to burn me. After all, hell hath no fury like a woman scorned!

Chapter Eight

Deshaun 'Grim' Jones

I COULD FEEL MY BODY URGING ITSELF TO WAKE UP. My legs had been twitching for some time now, and I felt my fingers wiggle.

Come on, I willed myself, and then my eyes began to roll before they flicked open. It took a few seconds for my eyes to focus. I looked around at the white hospital walls that held a small mounted TV and floral wall art. I dropped my head to look at my arm and saw that I was hooked up to an IV. I felt someone approach my bed, and when I looked up, it was Optimus. He was standing there smiling widely at me.

"Welcome back, nigga," he laughed, and I chuckled before coughing. My throat was dry and coarse.

"How long have I been here?" I asked in a deep raspy voice.

"Four days."

"How did you find me?"

"Kaliyah called me," he said, and I nodded. I'm glad she knew to call him and not the police.

"Where is she?" I asked.

"I don't know, Grim. She never came with us, and I haven't not seen her since," he said. I narrowed my brows at him.

"So, she called you, but she didn't come with you?"
I didn't understand that.

"Um... look, I think I scared her off from coming or something," he said, rubbing the back of his head with his left hand. He looked at the floor, avoiding my eyes, but I kept mine on him. After a while, he broke and looked up at me.

"I was just angry when I got there and saw you, G. She and Goldie were arguing over what happened, and I told her to pray that you didn't die, or I would kill her," he said. I shook my head at him.

"You threatened her?"

"A little, but it looked bad, Grim. You lost so much blood."

"She didn't hurt me on purpose, Optimus. She was fighting with Goldie. That bitch went into her room with a fucking knife. She started this whole shit!" I fumed.

"I fucking knew she had something to do with it. She kept telling me how Kaliyah just stabbed you like that," he said, and I shook my head. None of this would have happened if I had just stood my fucking ground and asked Goldie to leave.

"Do me a favor, Op. Call my parents, and let them know that I'm up. Go to my house, and get Kaliyah. I need to see her," I said, and he nodded. I had yet to tell my parents about her, but fuck it. They were going to find out about her sooner or later.

"Oh, and while you're there, grab Goldie's shit. I want her ass out of my fucking crib until I catch up to the bitch!" I growled. He nodded.

"That bitch has been here every-fucking-day, talking about she loves you," he told me, but I didn't even respond to him. She did the unforgivable by stepping to Kaliyah, and I would not let that shit go.

I heard the door being opened, and I looked up to see Goldie. She was creeping into the room, but her eyes bucked when she realized that I was looking right at her.

"Oh my God. You're awake!" she said with a shaky voice. She looked around the room nervously and started acting all jittery.

"What's the problem, Goldie? Why you are looking all nervous and shit?"

"Your parents were here earlier, so I left. I wasn't sure if they were still here or not," she said and smiled at me.

"I'm so glad you're awake now. I've been so worried about you," she said, looking at me. Optimus snorted, and I looked up at him.

"Come here, ma," I said, holding a hand out to her.

"I didn't think I would see you again," I said, and she slowly walked toward me. She stopped down by my feet, but I motioned with my hand for her to come closer, and she did.

She stopped near my hand, and I held it out to her. She looked up at me first and slowly dropped her hand in mine. When she did, I pulled her closer to me. I opened my arms wide to indicate that I wanted her to hug me, and when she leaned down toward me, I wrapped my hands around her throat instead.

"Didn't I fucking tell you not to try Kaliyah?" I grunted through clenched teeth and squeezed her neck.

"Did you think I was fucking playing? You went into her fucking room with a knife. Did you really believe I was going to let that shit go?"

I shook her as she fought to remove my hands from her throat.

"Believe when I say I'm going to snap your fucking neck

and end your life right here and now."

She looked at me with tears building in her eyes and her face red from the lack of oxygen.

"But she stabbed you, baby. I didn't," she croaked.

"None of this would have fucking happened if it wasn't for you!"

"So, you're not going to do anything about her almost killing you?" she choked, but stopped when I squeezed harder.

"No... because I love her, and she didn't mean to do it. Now shut the fuck up! I don't wanna hear none of your shit!"

"Op, call Trevor, and tell him to come and get this trash for me. I don't need the hospital all in my fucking business," I told Optimus, and he nodded. I released one of my hands from around her neck and slapped her across the face, but I tightened my hand that still held her throat to stop her scream from coming out. I wouldn't normally kill someone in a busy ass hospital like this, but fuck it. Goldie had to go!

Her eyes started to roll back as her life started to slip away from her, letting me know that I was ready to finally snap her neck and end her life. Because of the pressure I was applying to her throat, my injury started to hurt, and I suddenly felt like I was about to burst my stitches. I eased up slightly and pulled up the blanket just to check myself out. When I did that, she somehow pulled out of my grip and flew out of the door.

"Shit! Go and get her, nigga!" I yelled at Optimus, and he took off after her. My stitches were still intact, thankfully, because I wasn't trying to stay up in this bitch, but killing Goldie would have been worth it if they had burst. A few minutes later, Op walked back into the room without Goldie.

"She got away, Grim… my bad," he said, and I sucked my teeth.

"Call the niggas and put a price on her fucking head. I want that bitch
dead!"

She was the last fucking person to hurt Kaliyah and live to see another day.

"Without a doubt, G. The pussy was whack anyway."

He laughed and pulled out his phone to get on it. I slowly got out of the bed and headed to the bathroom to deal with my hygiene. I couldn't wait to see Kaliyah. I had missed her.

My dad wasn't going to like this at all, but I would deal with that when it came to it.

Chapter Nine

Deshaun 'Grim' Jones

"OH, MY GOD, BABY. YOU SCARED ME!" my mama hollered out and ran toward my bed as soon as she walked in. She rushed me and started kissing all over my face.

"Ma," I chuckled as she smothered me with her love.

"Welcome back, son," my pops said, laughing at my mother killing me with kisses.

"You would think that you're still a damn baby," he said, shaking his head. "He's my baby!" my mama told him straight, and I laughed.

"Can I get to my son too, Miriam?" he asked, and she huffed before moving out of the way. My pops leaned down and hugged me.

"What happened?" he asked, and I looked at my parents. I could never tell him that Kaliyah accidentally stabbed me. They would never understand, especially as my pops never wanted me to fall in love with anybody. He would use that as the perfect excuse to tell me to leave her alone. *Fuck these bitches. Give them your seeds, but don't fall in love...* his words, not mine.

"My friend was fighting, and I got in the middle of it. It was an accident that I'm dealing with," I said, and my pops nodded.

"Who was it? Tell me, and let me deal with it," my mama

said with her hands on her hips, causing me to laugh.

"Mama, it's cool. I've got it," I said, and she shook her head.

"So, I met your little girlfriend," she said, and my eyes bucked. I looked at my pops and he had a blank look on his face.

"I can't say that I like her at all," she continued as my heart raced. I knew I was grown, but I was close to my parents, and it would have been a living hell trying to be with Kaliyah when they didn't like her. I couldn't understand why! I was convinced that my mama would have liked her and could maybe help me convince my pops.

"I… I don't understand," I said, hoping she would elaborate on why she didn't like her without me giving anything away. I guess Kaliyah came when I was asleep, because Optimus was sure that she hadn't been here. He was due back any minute with her now. This was not going to end well.

"I never disliked piercings until I saw hers. I mean… who pierces their cheeks? It looks tacky to me," she said.

"Oh!" I said, bursting out laughing. Thank God, she was talking about Goldie.

"Mama, you ain't got to worry about Goldie. She is not my girl… never was and never will be," I said, and she smiled. *Plus, that bitch is gonna be dead soon,* I thought to myself.

"Good, because you already know what I was going to say… right, son?" my pops said, giving me a deep glare. I don't know why he was so adamant that I never fell in love and why he always said that he wished he never loved my mama so much. I wondered if that was why she had been looking sad for years.

My pops was not a forgiving man, so I already know that we

were going to bump heads about Kaliyah. I rubbed a hand over my face in a frustrated manner and sighed out.

Whenever my mama brought up me finding a wife and settling down, my pops always laughed it off in front of her, but when we were alone, it was almost like he forbade me to be in love. He tolerated me fucking around and never had an issue there, but love? He wasn't having it.

I admit that I wasn't sure what I wanted with Kaliyah up until we made love, but since having that near-death experience, I knew that I didn't want to spend another day without her. All I could do was hope my pops understood and allowed us to be together.

They spent a few hours with me before leaving, and I was surprised that Optimus hadn't arrived in that time. I didn't even have my cell phone on me. I wasn't sure where it was, so I couldn't even call him. Just as I was about to give up hope that he would arrive, he walked through the door looking lost.

"Yo, man, what the fuck took you so long?"

I laughed, looking behind him and expecting to see Kaliyah. "Where she at?" I asked, looking at him.

"I don't know, Grim... she's missing," he said, and my heart dropped. "WHAT DO YOU MEAN SHE'S MISSING?"

"She wasn't at your house when I got there, and she hasn't been to work in days. Not even Pedra knows where she is. I even went back to her mama's house, and she hasn't been back there since the night you found her. I've looked everywhere, and I can't find her, Grim. She's gone," he said, and I felt my soul leave my body.

Where the fuck was she?

Chapter Ten

Deborah 'Tuts' Diamond

I DIDN'T KNOW WHY THE FUCK Optimus was at my house looking for fucking Kaliyah. I bet the bitch fucked him too and ran off! I let him know that I didn't know where the bitch was, nor did I care. He never told me why he was looking for her, but good luck to her when he did find her, because he looked like he was going to kill her. This bitch had played me! The whole time, she acted like she hated going to the trap house, but she couldn't hate it that much if Optimus fucking knew her.

I don't know why, but my mind started fucking with me, telling me that the bitch was probably somewhere with Silvan! That's probably why his ass turned his phone off on me. They were together and had cheated me out of my money just like Simeon! That nigga took his ass down to the precinct and gave himself up like an idiot. He had the fucking police running all through my shit… bagging and tagging stuff and being all up in my business.

They were asking me where the fuck I was when my brother attacked her and why didn't I report it or protect her! I don'tknow who the fuck they thought they were, questioning me like that. This was what my daughter that I carried, birthed, and looked after did. This was her way of saying thank you!

"Are you proud now, Lester? Huh! The fucking daughter that you begged me to have, only for you to fucking leave me alone with her… are you proud of what she's become… with how she's fucked my life up?" I yelled out in my living room before chuckling to myself.

My mama was dead, my brother was in jail, and now my

daughter turned her back on me and left me for dead in this apartment alone while she lived it up like a fucking princess with ballers. Did she care if I had food or not! Of course, she didn't.

Pushing my feet in some slides, I grabbed my keys and rushed out of my house. They were not about to play me! I wanted my fucking money, and Silvan should have known better than to cross me. I marched to the train station and

barged my way onto the train towards 148th. I was so angry that I was seeing red. I never thought my daughter would snake me like that. She played me, because she really had me believing that she didn't like Silvan with her fake tears. How stupid could I have been? It was no coincidence that he disappeared a week after she left home. I bet they were laughing at me!

I sniffed and used the back of my hand to wipe my nose. I had not had a hit of anything in almost three days. I was fiending for it, but I had no money. My mama used to send money weekly to the house for Kaliyah, and that was how I was funding my habit, but she stopped once Simeon moved in, and he wouldn't give me any money after that point. He paid the bills, paid rent, and bought food, but he never ever handed me any money, because he already knew what I would do with it. Then, he got hooked on the stuff himself, leaving me free to his money until Kaliyah sent those niggas to my house.

Now, I was left begging friends for some, fucking other crackheads just to get a hit, and selling my furniture. The hate I felt for my daughter made my body feel like it was about to explode.

Getting off the train, I quickly made my way to the trap house. I expected to see Silvan outside, but I didn't. I did, however, recognize one short dark skinned nigga out there that I had seen with Silvan before.

I discreetly walked over to him and cleared my throat to get his attention.

He turned to look up at me and frowned. "Yes," he asked with an attitude.

"Where's Silvan? I've been calling him for weeks now," I said, shuffling on my feet. He looked left and right like he was making sure we were alone and then he stepped toward me.

"He's dead," he said and backed up away from me.

Oh my God!

Chapter Eleven

Deshaun 'Grim' Jones

THE DOCTORS TOLD ME THAT I NEEDED TO STAY a few more days in the hospital, but I wasn't trying to hear that. They said my ass wouldn't be out of the bed until hours after I woke up, but my ass was walking around minutes after. They weren't accustomed to dealing with a nigga like me! I didn't do weak shit.

My shit was repaired. I was no longer bleeding or in as much pain, so why the fuck did I need to stay? I needed to find Kaliyah. I needed to make sure her bitch ass mama or uncle didn't get a hold of her.

I climbed out of my hospital bed, went into the bathroom to shower, and put on the clothes that Optimus brought from my house. Once I was done, I brushed my teeth and brushed over my hair. I walked back into my room to see Demon fucking around with my bed, making it go up and down while Optimus and my cousin, Crew, argued over whose latest bitch was finer.

I slapped Demon on the back of his head to make him sit his ass down and started gathering up my shit to leave. A light knock came on my door, and that young-looking nurse walked in after I shouted for her to come in. She was cute in the face, but my baby was better, so I didn't even look over her that much. My niggas were watching her ass and trying to throw lines at her.

"I'm sorry about their thirsty asses." I chuckled, and she laughed.

"I got your discharge papers, even though the doctor advises you not to leave," she said, setting it down on the bed.

"Oh, and I'm not sure if you know this person, but a young girl came here. She was standing outside of your room asking questions. She said she didn't know you, but I think she did and was just scared for some reason," she said, and I looked at her.

"Was she small, pretty, and Blasian?" I asked. She nodded.

"Kaliyah," I said and smiled. I knew she would have come to see me.

There was just no way I could believe that she would just leave me like that. "When did she come here?"

"Two days ago," she said, walking back toward the door.

"I don't know why she was afraid to come in. You don't seem that bad."

She chuckled. I flicked my eyes up at Optimus who looked at me with his head down.

"Yeah, I wonder why she was so afraid," I said, and he didn't respond.

The nurse wished me luck and walked out of the room.

"Shit, Grim, how was I supposed to know that she would leave?" he finally said.

"What the fuck you mean? Maybe because a big ass King Kong looking motherfucker threatened to kill her!" I snapped, making Crew and Demon laugh.

"Shit, she could be hiding because of you too. You're the nigga called Grim… not me," he said while laughing, and I sucked my teeth at him. I zipped up my duffle bag and threw it at him for him to carry.

"Since you've got such a smart-ass mouth like a bitch, I'm gonna treat you like one," I said, and Demon choked laughing.

"That's all good, but you better buy my ass a meal before you fuck me, nigga," he said back, and we all fell out laughing. We left the hospital, and Crew went to get my Range from the parking lot. After I told him I was coming out of the hospital today, he went to my house and got it for me. He was my cousin and the only person I allowed to drive my shit.

A few minutes later, we all climbed in and Crew took off.

"Where have you looked for Kaliyah, Op?" I asked after taking a pull of the blunt Demon passed over to me. Crew was driving, and Optimus was up front with him.

"Everywhere that I could think of. I'm not sure if you ever noticed, butthat chick didn't go many places, so it wasn't like I had a lot of choices," he answered back.

"That's exactly why the fuck she's my girl. As soon as I find her, I'm locking her ass down," I said, and my niggas nodded their heads. Kaliyah was never out there like that, and that only made her more attractive to me.

"I'm still waiting for you to tell me exactly where you looked, nigga," I said to Op, and he started laughing.

"Oh yeah."

He coughed and passed his blunt to Crew.

"I went to her mama's, the building you found her in, her job, and Pedra's house. Nobody has seen her since the day before you got stabbed except her mama. She hasn't seen her since she ran away."

"At least she's not home with that fucked up woman and her shady ass brother," I snapped.

"Oh shit! I forgot to tell you, Grim… the niggas at the precinct said her uncle gave himself up for what he did to her," Demon said to me, and I nodded. "I'm glad, because I wanted to kill that nigga."

I took another pull of my blunt and closed my eyes. Optimus looked in the same places that I would have, and he was right. She didn't go many places, so I had no idea where to even look for her.

"Any word on Goldie?" I asked, because I hoped that she hadn't found Kaliyah alone, especially after I tried to kill her.

"No, she never went back to your place, because her shit was still there when I went looking for Kaliyah, but I threw it all out on the streets. She's not back at her mama's house either. Don't worry. We will find her," Optimus said.

"Yeah, I just hope the crazy bitch doesn't have Kaliyah or some shit like that. I mean… where the fuck is she?"

I was losing my fucking cool. Kaliyah didn't know anybody out there like that, so I couldn't understand where she could be.

"Hold up!" I suddenly shouted when I thought of something.

"Yo, Op, call Terrence. I want him to track her debit card," I instructed, and he did. I gave Terrence Kaliyah's debit card details since it was one of my accounts that I gave her to use when she got her job.

"Pull over," I told Crew, and he did.

"Terrence said her last transactions were at a motel," Optimus looked back and said to me.

"Where?"

"Galaxy motel… 860 Pennsylvania Avenue."

I didn't even have to say anything to Crew. He immediately

cranked up the car and did a U-turn before speeding to the motel.

I admit I was mad as fuck that she had to go to a shit hole like that, and I say that because a damn two-star motel wasn't shit compared to my houses. She shouldn't have even needed to go there in the first place. Optimus must have read my mind, because he looked up at me in the rear-view mirror.

"I'm gonna make it right," he said.

"I know you motherfucking will! Nigga, don't ever in your fucking life threaten my girl. I don't give a fuck. You hear me? She's not the one to play with. Trust me!" I said and he nodded. He had no business threatening her like that.

"Oh shit, cuz. You found your wife?"

Crew laughed as he swerved around cars. He was definitely my kin, because he drove the same fucked up way that I did.

"You better believe it! That's me, all day every-fucking-day!"

Chapter Twelve

Kaliyah Diamond

I HAD BEEN STAYING AT THIS MOTEL since I left Deshaun's house. I just googled and found a motel and took an Uber there. I felt so lonely staying in there. I missed Pedra and Deshaun so much. I was used to being alone. I had spent all my life alone, but since meeting them, I got used to having them around. I honestly thought that I would have been with them forever, I guess.

Man, I missed them something crazy, and I hoped that Deshaun was okay. I just knew that he was awake now and must have been mad, looking for me. I can't believe I almost killed him!

I dropped my head in my hands. I still had a little bit of money left, but it wouldn't last forever, and I couldn't just stay here in the motel. I couldn't go home, and I didn't want to, but maybe if I gave my mama the money I had left, we could try and work on being close. After all, she did what she did for money. Maybe now that I actually had some to offer her, it would change things.

"I had a job before. I could get another one easily. Plus, my manager didn't want me to leave, so she told me to call her if I ever wanted my old job back," I spoke to myself as I packed up the little belongings I had to go home, trying to tell myself that this wasn't a bad idea. I'd heard what my uncle said, but I didn't have a choice at this moment. My money would not last forever, and I couldn't afford to pay for a room and food.

Once I was all packed, I put my backpack on and left the room.

I handed my keycard back to reception and walked out of the entrance. As soon as my feet touched down outside, I saw a car parked outside with Deshaun, Optimus, and two other men that I didn't know, inside.

"Oh my God!" I yelped and took off running.

"Kaliyah!!" I heard Deshaun's voice as I ran for my life. *He's going to kill me! He's going to kill me,* I thought as I ran. I heard feet behind me, but I was too scared to look back. When I felt a big hand grab me, I screamed at the top of my lungs.

"Calm down, Kaliyah," I heard, and I looked up to see that Optimus had picked me up.

"Please, I didn't mean it! I wasn't trying to hurt him! I promise!" I screamed.

"Yo, stop all that fucking screaming before someone calls the police on my big ass, K. I won't be impressed if that happens," he said to me, and I quietened down out of fear.

Completely helpless, I watched as Optimus carried me back to the car. I started to cry as I saw Deshaun standing outside of the car.

"Please, Deshaun, I'm so sorry. I never meant to hurt you. Please don't kill me, please. It was an accident. I swear."

I balled my eyes out. Optimus put me down on my feet right in front of Deshaun. I jumped out of my skin when I felt Deshaun grab me into a hug.

"Baby, I would never hurt you," he said into my ear, and I broke down. "I thought I killed you!" I wailed as he held me close.

"I was so scared."

I continued to sob. I held onto him for dear life as I took in his wonderful scent that I missed so much.

"Kaliyah, I told you I would never ever hurt you. Why would you think that I would kill you? Why would you run away from me?"

He pulled me back and looked at my face. He thumbed my tears away and kissed my lips.

"Because Pedra told me that you killed someone because they punched you. Imagine what you would do with me after that happened…"

I sniffled, and he chuckled.

"Plus…" I turned around and looked at Optimus. I didn't want to snitch, but he did tell me he would kill me himself.

"Plus, this big ass nigga told you he would kill you, right?" Deshaun said, laughing with his other friends. I slowly nodded my head as I kept my eyes on Optimus. He really was a big scary looking man, and his deep voice didn't help.

"Apologize, blood," one of the other men said to Optimus. I turned to look at him, and he favored Deshaun in the face with the same dark glossy eyes. Everybody turned around to face Optimus. He bent down to my level so that we were face to face.

"I apologize, Kaliyah. I didn't mean it." He smiled at me.

"Now, slap his face," the white looking man said. I snapped my head back at Optimus and shook my head no.

"Go ahead. He ain't about to do shit about it," Deshaun said, lifting my hand for me.

"You better take your chance," Optimus said, and I smiled before pulling my hand back and slapping the shit out of him.

"DAMMMMNNNNN!" everybody hollered out before falling into fits of laughter. I even chuckled a little, because I didn't think I would have slapped him that hard. Optimus just looked at me and shook his head before standing up straight again. I turned to face Deshaun again when I felt him tugging on my shoulder.

"I missed you, and I'm sorry about Goldie."

He stepped closer to me and kissed my lips again.

"So, this is my cousin-in-law?" the man who looked like him asked while smiling down at me.

"Yep," Deshaun said and nodded.

"Baby, this is my cousin, Crew. Crew… meet my baby, Kaliyah," he said, introducing us. I shook his hand, and we smiled at each other. Deshaun wrapped his arms around me and hugged me tightly.

"Let's go home, baby," he said, but I shook my head no. I didn't want to go back to that house after everything that had happened. I suspected that his blood was probably still on my bedroom floor, and I didn't want to see it.

Deshaun must have felt my worries as his own because kissing my cheek, he said, "don't worry, baby. We're never going back to that house."

I fell into his warm embrace, and he kissed the top of my head. He took my backpack and opened the car door for me. I climbed in as everybody else did. Deshaun kept a hand on my knee as we made our way to his main house. His cousin and friends were so funny. They cracked jokes about each other the whole way there. The white looking guy told me his name was

Demon, and they laughed after seeing my face. I mean… who calls their self Demon?

When we pulled up outside, grabbing my backpack, I smiled at everybody and said good bye as I climbed out of the car. Deshaun slapped hands with them before taking me by the hand and leading me into the house. As soon as he closed the door, he swooped me up into his arms and carried me into the bedroom as our mouths became acquainted with each other again. He kissed me deeply and feverishly before laying me down on his bed.

"I missed the hell out of you, Kaliyah. I know now that I want to be with you more than anything," he said, stroking my face and kissing me again.

"You wanna be my lady?" he asked me against my lips, and I laughed. "Yes, Deshaun. I think I love you," I whispered, and he looked at me. "No… I know that I do," I finally admitted.

"I love you more, baby."

He kissed me again. I wrapped my arms around his neck as we deepened the kiss. He pulled my T-shirt over my head and threw it down. I did the same to him after. I hummed as he kissed down my neck and over my breasts that he quickly released by unclipping my bra.

"Mmmm," I cooed as he sucked on a nipple. He pushed my tights down my legs as he trailed kisses down my body. Licking his lips, he pulled my panties down and off. He spread my legs as far as they would go, and I shivered when I felt his warm tongue lick my middle.

"Don't be scared," he said, and I nodded. This was the first time that someone put their mouth on me since Silvan and Zoe forced it on me, but as his tongue gently swiped over every inch of me, I cried out of pure pleasure. They had scarred that interaction for me, but Deshaun kissed that away with every stroke his tongue gave me.

"Uhhhhhh."

I arched my back, and my body stiffened as a wave of orgasmic pleasure washed over me. I heard him grunt in pleasure, and it made me gush that much more. After taking me over the edge for another round, he gently kissed his way up my body. I looked into his eyes as he thumbed my tears away. I was so glad that I never killed him.

Our mouths crushed together again, and I whimpered when I felt his hugeness filling me up and stretching my walls.

"Damn, Kaliyah," he muttered against my ear. He hooked my legs into the crook of his arms and pushed deeper into me.

"Ahhhh!" I cried and dug my nails into his back. Circling his hips into me, he bit and sucked my collarbone. Once I was adjusted to his size again, I couldn't control the moans that escaped from my mouth. He picked up his pace and started beating it up, making our skin slap loudly against each other.

"You're so fucking wet, K," he grunted. My eyes rolled back, and I bit down on my bottom lip as he pumped rapidly, hitting my spot. I could feel my wetness on the inside of my thighs, and it made gushing sounds with each thrust that he seemed to like. He sucked and licked across my breasts for a while before pulling out of me.

"Get on your knees, baby… head down, ass up," he instructed, looking at me with low eyes as he bit down on his lip.

I did as he asked and had to bury my face into a pillow to mask my scream as he drilled his way back into me.

"Damn, Kaliyah!" he yelled out. I bucked rapidly as he pumped away into me. He circled his hips deep into me as he bent over to kiss, suck, and gently bite on my shoulder and back. With one hand gripping my hair and another holding my hip, he bounced me on his rod.

"Ahhhhh, Deshaun!"

"You're mine forever, Kaliyah. Do you hear me? You're mine, baby," he said in a raspy voice.

"Yes… I'm… yours," I panted each word out, unable to speak from the pleasure he was giving me. I jumped when I felt him slap my ass, but I kind of liked it.

"Bounce back against me, baby. Throw that ass back," he said, and I started pushing back, meeting his thrusts.

"Yes, fuck! That's it. I'm gonna nut!" he growled just as I felt myself release, coating my thighs as it ran down.

"Shit! Fuck! SHIITTTTT!" he grunted loudly until I felt him pump so fast into me I had to hold on to the comforter so that I wouldn't fall off the bed. Seconds later, he shook and collapsed on top of me, making us both drop down flat on the bed. Damn! We had never had sex like that before, and I loved every second of it. I know he was gentle with me the first time, but I preferred this, despite my throbbing vagina.

After a few seconds, he planted a few kisses on my neck, shoulder, and back before pulling himself out of me. He rolled onto his back, and I turned my head to look at him.

"I bought this for you," he said, going into the side table drawer and pulling out a chain. I gasped with a big smile on my face.

"Just a token of my appreciation for you. Promise me that you will never ever take it off," he said, and I promised that I wouldn't. I leaned forward, giving him access to fasten it around my neck. When it was done, I held it and looked down at it. The pendant was so pretty and was a K.

"Deshaun!" I yelped when I felt his strong arms lift me into the air. "Let's shower and eat something so that I can beat that pussy up again." He laughed and kissed me.

Damn! I found me a street king!

Chapter Thirteen

Deshaun 'Grim' Jones

HAVING KALIYAH BACK HOME WITH ME felt so damn good. It had been almost two weeks since I found her, and I spent it fucking the hell out of that girl! She had the snuggest, wettest, and sweetest pussy I had ever encountered, and I was without a doubt pussy-fucking-whipped! She had a nigga wide open. That was for sure.

My pops finally had a hit for me, so I was on my way to meet him at the warehouse. I put Kaliyah to sleep before I left, making me smile when I remembered how she tapped out, begging for mercy. Don't for a second feel sorry for her, because little miss pretty ass broke the hell out of her shell. She'd been riding the fuck out of my dick, making me cry like a bitch. Trust and believe, if she got on top, it was all over! That pussy would lock me in a tight ass chokehold, bringing tears to my eyes, so she wasn't that innocent anymore!

On the outside, we probably didn't look like we matched each other, but thug or not, I can say that we matched each other perfectly. She was the perfect balance in my life which I needed in my line of work. If I wasn't on a hunt or kill, I was dealing with the trap houses and shit. That brought out Grim and a constant angry version of myself. It felt good being able to switch that off and chill with K.

That's another reason why I couldn't even think about getting serious with Goldie. She constantly added to my stress, and knowing me, I would have fucked around and killed her sooner or later. She was like a fucking Chihuahua... always yapping at the damn mouth, and with my ignorant side, it wouldn't have worked.

I had a softer side that I reserved only for my mama, because that was my heart, but it felt good that I had another person in my life who got to share that part of me. Just seeing Kaliyah's face calmed my ass down. She was exactly what I needed. It was just a shame I couldn't tell my pops about her.

Speaking of Goldie, I still hadn't found that bitch yet! It was like she disappeared somewhere, but I knew her well enough to know that sooner or later, her ass would show up, and I would gladly kill her ass then! When I arrived at my pop's warehouse, he was standing outside, leaning up against his black on black Range and smoking a fat ass blunt. He nodded his head at me when I pulled up alongside him. I grabbed my Blaser rifle and climbed out.

"What up?" he said to me, giving me a one shouldered hug and a fist pound.

"You good?" I asked as I looked around.

"Yeah, and I will be better once this meeting is over. You know what to do, don't you?" he asked me, and I nodded. There wasn't anything else left to say, because I wasn't there for a social meeting. I was on a job. I dapped my pops and headed for my location which was on the roof. I set my gun up and cracked open the roof window.

I smiled to myself as I sat and thought about Kaliyah as I smoked on a blunt. She really had transformed from that scared little girl that I found in that building months back. She was now this bubbly, talkative, sweet, kind, and funny person who lit up the whole room with her presence.

Her mama was a damn fool. She had the best daughter and

didn't even realize it. Kaliyah should have been someone that her mama should have been proud of, but her loss was my gain. Without Kaliyah's mother being such a fucked up woman, I would have never met Kaliyah.

I chuckled when I remembered how she woke me up this morning, trying to give me some head. She was all about trying to please me, and that made me love her that much more, because her focus was on me and not niggas in general. I was scared to fall in love. I never thought that I would, but I'm glad I took that chance with her.

The sound of cars approaching the warehouse cut my thoughts short. I stumped out my blunt and crawled to the edge of the rooftop to look down at the cars. Six cars in total had pulled up.

"Let's get this out of the way," I whispered to myself and crawled back over to my gun. I looked down through my scope, and my dad was looking up at me. He gave me a head nod to let me know that he was ready. The warehouse doors opened, and in walked six powerful men. They were the heads of their crime organizations outside of New York, and my pops called a meeting, because he wanted to merge their businesses together. When I say merge, I meant he wanted to take over. That's what he did. He didn't co-exist with anybody. He took it all.

I zoned in on James. He was the head of an organization in Delaware that dealt with diamonds. He had successfully pulled off over a hundred heists from all over the world. He had a team of experts underneath him.

My pops came across his name when he was on the last business trip he took to Germany. Out of the six men, he was my father's biggest thorn in his side, because he wasn't about to just allow my pops a piece of his pie, so to speak. That's why I was here!

"Gentlemen…"
My father's loud voice echoed.

"Welcome to New York," he said with his arms outstretched. The men gave back a quick response before taking a seat in the chairs that were laid out before my pops. James, who looked a lot like Common, unbuttoned his blazer and fixed his eyes on my pops. I wanted to shoot that nigga just from the way he was looking at my dad.

"Now, I'm a man about my money, so I will get straight to the point, because every second that I stand here, I could be making money."

My pops smirked at them, and they nodded their heads.

"I called this meeting to discuss our families merging," he said, and the men began looking amongst each other. Even though they were all heads of separate organizations, it seemed that James was somehow the one to follow which is why he was my dad's biggest threat. It was like they wouldn't do anything without James' input, and the way the other five were looking at him proved what we had been hearing in the streets. Not fazed by the looks he was getting from James, my pops continued.

"I know some very important people, and I have connections all over the world which will benefit you. Imagine just walking into another country and getting what you want without anybody even knowing you were there? I have people in official places who can do that, instead of you having your people travel on fake identification to get in and out like you have been doing. I can get hold of merchandise that nobody else has… shit… stuff that most people don't even know have been made."

He chuckled, pushing a cigar into his mouth. My pops wasn't lying there. He had people in his pockets that worked in places like the Army, the Pentagon, even Parliament in the United Kingdom! There wasn't a place on the earth that he didn't have somebody working. He didn't have to worry about the police, officials, or airport security. He was that well connected.

The men looked around at each other again and looked back at James. "And what are you looking for in return, Pattison?" James finally spoke up and asked.

"I want to be the head, and I want forty-five percent out of everything that you make," my pops said, puffing on his cigar.

"Like hell! I'm the motherfucking head of my shit and nobody else! I ain't going into partnership with you!" James yelled and pointed at my dad.

"I'm not asking for a partnership. If I'm the head, how the fuck can we be partners?" my dad snarled at him.

"I would rather die," James said.

"It would be in your favor if you joined me, James."

They all looked at James for a response. I don't even know why my pops wanted to work with such pussy ass niggas who couldn't talk for their damn selves, but he had a plan. I knew he did. Otherwise, he wouldn't have wasted his time with them.

"You think that you can just come in and take over what we fucking worked hard for?" James growled and instinctively, my finger went on the trigger.

"I don't think I can, James. I know that I can. You would be wise to fall into place."

My pops was so cool and collected when he said that, but I knew deep down inside, he was probably raging.

"Fuck you!" James spat, and my pops chuckled. "Gentlemen..."

My dad turned his attention to the other men.

"I'm going to give you one chance to accept my offer, and James... this is my final warning to you."

James shook his head, laughing, and the other men didn't even respond. "Pattison, go and fuck yourself!" James said.

"What the fuck can you do? There's six of us and one of you!"

"Wrong answer," my dad said and nodded, so I let off one shot right into James' head, and it almost blew off his shoulders. The other men jumped back just as James' lifeless body crashed to the floor. My dad was acting cool as fuck like a dead body wasn't only inches away from his feet.

"Now, gentlemen... you can either walk out of here with your lives, and I take everything from you, or join me, but I'm taking over with or without you. James' spot was already mine. His people are already underneath me, but I was trying to give him a chance of still making some money, and he never took it."

"I'm in!" they all shouted out almost simultaneously.

"I bet y'all are, but because you wanted to test my authority, I will now take sixty-five percent from you instead of my initial offer."

My pops smiled at them. Damn, he was ruthless, but I had to

respect his hustle. The man agreed to my pops' terms and left, but not before my pops made them take James' body with them. Once I saw that they had all left, I got down from the roof. My pops had a smile on his face, and all I could do was laugh and dap him up.

"I can always rely on you, son."

He smiled and handed me an envelope of money. With my own smile on my face, I headed out to my car. I left him at the warehouse and thought I would check in with my mama before going home to my girl. I should have told my pops about Kaliyah, but shit... I was too happy with her to fuck it up by telling him. He didn't mind me fucking bitches and breaking off a seed or two to carry on my legacy, but loving them, spending money on them, and other shit, he openly forbade me to do. I wasn't afraid of my pops. I just didn't want the trouble coming mine and Kaliyah's way... not now anyway.

I used my keys to let myself in when I got to my parents' house. The lights were out, except for a light in the den. I walked toward the door, and my mama was sitting on the couch with a brown throw over her body, and she had her face buried in a photograph.

"Son," she said when she looked up and saw me standing there. She quickly pushed the photo behind her back so that I couldn't see it.

"What was that you were looking at?"

"Oh... nothing important, son... just some old photos I found and need to throw out."

She smiled, and I noticed that her eyes were unusually glossy and red, letting me know that she had been crying.

"Mama, why do you hide things from me? Don't you trust me

to help you?" I asked, and her face softened. She motioned with her hand for me to come closer to her, and when I did, I kneeled in front of her. She kissed my cheek and ran a hand down my face.

"I trust you with my life, Shaun, and I know that you would help me, but this isn't anything that you can help with. Somebody I knew died, and every time the anniversary comes around, it makes me emotional, but I am okay, baby. I promise," she said and kissed me again. "Now, let me feed you."

She smiled and went to stand, so I moved back. She pulled the throw off her body and grabbed the photo that she had tucked down the side of the chair. I shook my head and chuckled to myself. I was hoping she left it so that I could look at it, but she was one step ahead of me.

Chapter Fourteen

Kaliyah Diamond

PEDRA AND I WERE JUST GETTING BACK after spending the day out shopping. We hit up all types of places, and I had to even venture to 125th Street, because Pedra had ordered something from H&M and it went to that store on an error. I won't lie and say that my heart wasn't racing the whole time, because I had not been back in that area since the night I left, but we didn't stick around which I was grateful for. I had not explained what happened that night.

It wasn't that I didn't trust Pedra, because I did. She and I had grown very close, but how do you tell someone that your uncle raped you, and your mama tried to sell your virginity for money so that she could buy some drugs? That's not something I wanted to ever tell a soul, and I know if I didn't have all that Hennessy in my body that night, I wouldn't have told Deshaun either. Pedra knew my mama and I didn't get along, and that she used to beat on me, but that's all I had explained to her. Maybe one day I would be strong enough to tell her everything.

We dropped our bags in the living room and sighed out when our aching butts hit the plush couch.

"Damn, I didn't think we would have been out that long!" Pedra said, and I nodded my head to agree. We initially said that we would be out for maybe two hours, but we ended up being out there for almost five hours! We left my house at 11 o'clock in the morning, and it was now after 6 o'clock in the evening. After resting my tired ass for a few minutes, we both got up and headed to the kitchen for something to drink. Before I could even open the refrigerator, the doorbell rang.

I looked at Pedra like I expected her to know who was at the damn door. Nobody had ever come over here since Deshaun and I moved here. I wasn't sure whether to get it or not, because I knew that Deshaun had keys.

"Bitch, you ain't gonna get that?"

Pedra looked at me and I shook my head no.

"Nobody should know this house. Deshaun told me that no one knew he even had this house. Maybe somebody has the wrong house," I said just as the buzzer went again.

"Hmmmm, maybe it's a bitch! If it is, let's beat her ass!" Pedra said, punching a fist into her hand.

"Okay, Deshaun said I was the only female he ever brought here, and I'm not beating anybody else."

"Okay… you watch, and I will," she said, and we started laughing. The person was persistent and continued to ring the doorbell. I decided to go and open it just in case it was Deshaun and he had left his keys. With Pedra right behind me, I crept to the door and pulled it open.

"MAMA?"

I blinked my eyes rapidly, hoping that I was dreaming, but as I looked at my mama's angry face, I knew that I wasn't. She stood there looking at me with all the hate her body could muster up, and everything she ever did to me came flashing back. She didn't smile or greet me. She just pushed past me into the house.

I turned back to look at Pedra before I reluctantly closed the front door and followed my mama. She was walking and looking around with a shake of her head, and every few seconds, she would suck her teeth loudly. Once she had enough of taking it all in, she walked into the living room and sat on the couch. I slowly approached and sat on the couch opposite from her. She sat looking at me with her mouth curled up in the corner, and it was a look of disgust.

"So, you mean to tell me that while I'm sitting in that fucking cockroach infested house, you're out here living the high life?" she yelled at me.

"Bitch, you didn't even fucking look for my girl, so shut your old ass up!" Pedra snapped at her. My mama didn't even pay attention to her and acted like she wasn't even in the room.

"Mama, how—"

"How did I find you?" she completed my question for me. Snorting, she continued.

"I followed your ass when I saw you going into H&M on 125th."

I looked at Pedra. We were both worried about going back to my old area, but we thought we could get in and out quickly enough.

"You lied to me, Kaliyah, and used me! How could you leave like that and leave me behind after every-fucking-thing that I did for you?"

"Mama, how did I use you?"

"Bitch! You lived in my fucking house rent free for almost eighteen damn years! When you had enough, you moved on to your own lavish life! Look at the fucking house you're living in!"

She flapped her arms about.

"This fucking couch that I'm sitting on costs more than all the furniture in my house."

"Uh, that's called being a fucking mother! You are supposed to provide shit for your kids," Pedra said and shook her head.

"I thought that maybe this little dark skinned hoe that you're with lived here, but I knew once I saw you open the door with the keys."

"Who the fuck are you calling a hoe, you coke head bitch?" Pedra yelled and tried to run at her, but I pulled on her arm and stopped her.

"I see you're still telling people my fucking business, Kaliyah! But you are far from perfect! Whose dick are you sitting on to be living this life of money? I bet it's Silvan, isn't it… or Optimus' big ass! You're a little fucking whore, Kaliyah, and I should have fucking swallowed your ass or aborted you!"

She jumped to her feet.

"AYE! GET THE FUCK OUT OF MY HOUSE, BITCH!"

We all jumped when we heard Deshaun's voice roar out. I was so busy arguing with my mama that I didn't even hear him coming into the house. My mama dropped back on the couch and looked at him like she was seeing a ghost or something.

"You ain't about to talk to my fucking girl like that! Get the fuck out!" he yelled at her as he approached me.

"You okay, baby?"

He stroked my cheek, and I nodded yes. I was so over my mother and her hate for me that what she was saying didn't trouble me at all. A few months ago, the old Kaliyah would have cowered and cried from her words, but this new Kaliyah had been through a lot of shit, and I was still standing! Gone were the days when my mama broke me down.

"Your girl?"

My mother stood to her feet with her mouth wide open and stared at us. "Grim... how? But... w-whhy? What are you doing with my daughter?" she asked him.

"Your fucking daughter? Was she your daughter when you were selling her to fucking niggas from my trap house? Was she your daughter when I found her fucking sleeping in an abandoned building after running away from your fucked up ass?" he roared at her.

"Your trap house? I thought it was Silvan's." She ran her hand over her face.

"Oh my God. What did I do?"

Deshaun and I both looked at each other and then at her. *What was she talking about?*

"Grim, please! You can't be with her!" she said and rushed toward me, pulling on my arm.

"We have to leave right now!"

She pulled me, but Deshaun pushed her off of me.

"Don't fucking touch her! She's not going anywhere with you! Now, get the fuck out before I beat your fucking ass, Tuts!"

He stepped in front of me and glared down at her.

"You don't understand, Grim! You cannot be with her! You have no idea what this would do or mean. You don't know who you're with!" she screamed, but he grabbed her by the arm and dragged her toward the door.

"Listen to me!" she challenged him, but he opened the door and pushed her out.

"I know exactly who I'm with, and she's not a coked-out hoe like you!" I heard him yell at her. I walked slowly toward the door and looked down at my mom. I was sad to see that our relationship led us to the point that she was being thrown out of a home that I lived in, but she made this relationship the way it was. I forgave her for what she did, but I would never forget.

"If you bring your ass back here again, I'm going to kill you," Deshaun said, and she looked at me like I was going to say something about it, but I didn't. I gave my mother more than enough chances, and she did nothing but hurt me.

I looked at her one last time before I turned around and walked back into the living room. That chapter of my life was done, and I knew at that point that I would never see that woman again if I could help it.

Chapter Fifteen

Deborah 'Tuts' Diamond

I COULDN'T BELIEVE THAT GRIM of all people was with my damn daughter! I couldn't believe that little bitch left me to die alone in that fucking rundown apartment while she lived the life of a queen. I was shocked as hell when I was walking down 125th trying to get a hit of somebody's shit, since I had no money, and I saw her ass! It angered me that she was out there spending money while I was barely eating any fucking food. I figured that from the shopping bags she had in her hands.

Even though I was told by that ugly nigga that Silvan was dead, I didn't believe it. I thought he just had people tell me that so that I would stop fucking looking for him. I just knew that Kaliyah was somewhere with him, and seeing her with money like that just confirmed my suspicions. I decided to follow her and confront their asses, but what I wasn't expecting was to see her with Grim! Damn, the house was fucking beautiful, and that only heightened the anger and jealousy that I felt for my daughter.

How the fuck did she end up with Grim? My fuck up caused this, and now things were about to get fucking real! I used to get my shit from a kid in my building but he had gotten killed. I asked around and found out that he was from

the trap house on 148th. I went down there, and that's when I first met Silvan. He told me it was his trap house, and I believed him. Had I had known it was really Grim's, I would have never fucking sent Kaliyah there, and I damn sure wouldn't have let her run away. My actions caused this, and now, my life would definitely be in danger if it wasn't already.

I tried to warn her, but she wanted to listen to Grim's ass instead of me! Well, good luck to her. As for me, I needed to get my ass out of New York and fast. The only problem was that I had no fucking money.

"The bitch couldn't even break me off a few dollars for good measure! She just let that nigga put me out like that? Well, when they are both dead, nobody will shed a got damn tear for either of them," I mumbled to myself as I made my way from their house back into Harlem. I can't believe that I had followed Kaliyah over an hour on the trains just to be put out like that! Fuck them! Oh, and it was no secret who fucking killed Silvan!

I was fucking angry that I was fiending for a damn hit. I went down to the trap house to look for that little ugly nigga who used to fuck with Silvan. Hopefully, I could put the charm on, and he would give me a little hit of something along with a few dollars so that I could get the bus out of town.

"My mama is dead, my brother is rotting in jail, and my other daughter is in a mad house. All I had was Kaliyah, and she fucking left me all alone. Now, my life was in danger because of her!" I grumbled to myself as I walked down the street. There was nothing left for me in Harlem now, but I was going to be just fine.

I was so happy to see his little ass when I got out there. He was sitting on the steps, talking to two other niggas that I didn't know.

"Ahem," I said, clearing my throat, trying to get their attention because they were being loud, laughing, and talking about a female who had walked past with a fat ass.

"Hello!" I shouted when nobody acknowledged me standing there. He finally looked up at me and sucked his teeth.

"You again? What you want?" he asked in an annoyed tone and walked over to me. He turned his head to watch that girl disappear down the street before looking over at me again.

"Look, can you help me out with a little something? Silvan used to all the time, but he's not around anymore… just a little something, and you won't see me again," I whispered to him. I had to let him know, because after this, I was out of here. My mama had a sister who lived in North Carolina, and that bitch didn't send a fucking dime when I told her my mama died, so she owed me!

"And if you have a few dollars to spare, I would appreciate that."

I smiled at him and licked my lips. He was an ashy looking nigga, so I knew he couldn't be getting much play from bitches. If I had to fuck him for a hit and $100 dollars, then I would.

"Aye, listen… I don't want anything you have to offer, Tuts. I know about that ran through pussy."

He laughed in my face, and my jaw dropped.

"That 'currency' isn't accepted around here," he coughed out while laughing.

"And besides… Grim has banned us from serving you, so you gotta leave."

"WHAT?" I yelled in shock. I was just out here last night getting some shit with my last amount of money and didn't anybody say anything about being banned then. Why the fuck was I banned now?

"He just told us an hour ago not to give you any fucking thing again, so bounce before I put my foot up your ass. I ain't getting murked over your hoe old ass pussy!" he snarled and pushed me away from him. I went to say something else, but he lifted his T-shirt and pulled his gun from his waist. I looked behind him to see the other niggas he was talking to had all done the same thing.

"Fuck y'all, Grim, and my bitch ass daughter!" I spat and hurriedly walked away. I knew that Kaliyah told Grim to do that, because I had never been banned before! It's okay though. Once everybody found out that they're together, she was gonna wish she had listened to me.

"Fuck 'em," I fumed and made my way toward the train station.

"Hello, pretty lady," a tall man with a chocolate complexion walked up to me and said. I looked him up and down. He was handsome enough with a gold watch glistening on his wrist. I smiled and licked my lips. Maybe I could worm a few hundred dollars out of him and get myself a bus ticket.

"Where you off to? Can I give you ride somewhere?" he asked as his eyes landed on my hips. I giggled when he bent his neck around trying to look at my ass. *Damn, he wasn't even subtle with this shit.*

"Like what you see?" I asked with a smile. "Yep."
He licked his lips.

"What would I have to do to get a lady like you to give me some good stuff?"

I usually had to approach the niggas I fucked with, but seeing him act so thirsty after me had my pussy jumping with anticipation. I hadn't fucked anybody since I fucked with Simeon's crack head friend last week.

"Well, what you willing to give me?" He wasn't about to hit this for free.

"$300 dollars."

He smiled and flashed me a roll of cash. Shit, that was better than the fifty dollars I was hoping to get from ugly.

"Where?" I asked, and he smiled at me.

"I have a hotel. Come… my car is just over there."

He walked away, and I followed. I was definitely going to work my magic in NC. Fuck everybody and Kaliyah too. I didn't need that bitch to make money. I could do fine on my own.

I watched the stranger as he strutted toward his car. At least I would enjoy this fuck, because he wasn't bad looking at all. He didn't seem like a coke head or anything. My eyes lit up when I saw him unlock a fucking Benz.

"Have you ever been to North Carolina?" I asked as I climbed into his car. Damn, he could come and see me any time! He chuckled and started the car. I closed my eyes and enjoyed the feeling of the fresh leather underneath my ass.

"What the fuck are you doing?" I screamed when I felt arms behind me grabbing on me. I was so interested in getting this money that I didn't even check if anybody else was in the car. I went to scream at the top of my lungs, but something was held over my mouth, and before I knew it, I was out cold.

***

When I opened my eyes again, I didn't know what was going on. I found myself inside some kind of hot ass shipping container. I looked around to see it was packed with women who all looked as scared as I was.

"What the fuck is going on?" I yelled and jumped up to my feet. I rushed to the container doors and tried my hardest to push it open. I could feel the tears building behind my eyes as I used all the strength I had.

"LET ME OUT!"

I banged and kicked at the metal doors. "Shhhhh," a slim Asian woman called out to me.

"You don't want them to come in here. It won't be good," she said, and when I looked her over, I noticed her lip was busted, and her eyes were black.

"Why are we even in here?" I asked her since nobody else looked like they wanted to talk to me.

"We are being sold, lady. They are sex traffickers. You got picked up by one," she said, and my body went stone cold.

"Wait, what?" I asked, and she nodded. I didn't want to hear what she had to say, so I tried again to push open the doors, but it wouldn't move at all. Where the doors met, it made a little slit, and I pushed my face flat against it to see if I could see anything, but it was pitch black outside, and I could swear we were on the water somewhere.

Defeated, I slid down the door and thumped on the ground. Tears flowed down my cheeks. *How did my life get to this point?*

I sat and thought about it all, and only one thing led me here…my daughter!

MAN, I HATED MY DAUGHTER!

Chapter Sixteen

Deshaun 'Grim' Jones

MY ASS WAS BEYOND TIRED. I had been out all day dealing with shit with my boys and my cousin, Crew. Word on the streets was that some niggas had been scoping out our trap houses like they wanted to do something. They were under the impression that they were going to rob my pops and live to talk about it.

I put everybody up to the game and let it be known that if any of the trap houses were hit, every fucking person inside was being murked, so they had better be on their toes. So far, it seemed like they were just watching the shit, trying to learn our movements or something, but I made a choice to roll up on those niggas first before they even had the chance.

See, I wasn't a nigga who allowed shit to happen first and then retaliate. I hit first to let motherfuckers know that I wasn't the one to play with. I guess these niggas didn't know about me.

Because I had sent word to our workers about what was going on, they were more watchful, and one of them was able to take a photo of the niggas in their car watching our spot. He sent me it to me, and let's just say, my ass tracked those niggas down. I was about five minutes from their spot. I had a few niggas sit on their location, and we knew they were cruising around in their whip. I checked the chamber of my two gold Desert Eagle handguns that I had my name engraved on.

"You ready, cuz?" Crew asked me as he crept his car toward those niggas.
"Yep."

I nodded my head. I looked out of the window and peeped those lame ass niggas leaning against the car, smoking and drinking.

"Stupid ass motherfuckers," I grumbled under my breath. You can't be caught slipping when you are planning to rob somebody. They were out there celebrating like they had already hit us up.

"Pull over," I told Crew, and he did. They hadn't even noticed that we had pulled over not far from them. The four of us climbed out and split into two, just in case someone tried to run. Demon and I approached from in front of them, and Crew and Optimus walked further down the street to then cross over and come up behind them.

My eyes zoned in on the leader who was a tall and skinny nigga who had his back turned to me. Without any warning, I pulled my two guns out and trained one on him and the other at one of his four men's head, just as Optimus and Crew walked up with theirs drawn. The skinny dude turned to look at me, and he reminded me of Fetty Wap with the same fucked up eye but just darker and minus the hair.

"So, you motherfuckers thought that y'all could run up in my spot to rob me and think that y'all were gonna get away with it?" I yelled. The other men looked around at us and then turned their eyes on their so-called leader like he was about to do something.

"Motherfucker, you obviously don't know who the fuck I am! Who sent you, nigga?"

I pressed my gun into the forehead of Pussy Wap. He was chewing on his bottom lip, showing that he was angry, but he never said a word.

"Oh, you ain't wanna talk? I bet your boys will though," I chuckled out.

"No, they won't. We ain't telling you shit, nigga!"

He tried to act hard. Still chuckling, I let loose one head shot to one of his niggas, and his body dropped to the floor with a loud thump. Instantly, his boys started singing like birds.

"I ain't dying for that hoe, Goldie!" a young -looking nigga yelled out, and that shit got my attention.

"Goldie?" I questioned and fell out laughing. *Shit! That's where that bitch went!*

"Nigga, you came after me over a bitch?" "Man, don't call my bitch no bitch!" he spat.

"Yo' bitch? Nigga, she was everybody's bitch! Both my homey and I smashed that hoe!"

I pointed at Optimus who nodded his head while laughing.

"Me too!" Demon suddenly called out, and I looked at him before laughing.

"Nigga, when did you fuck her?" I quizzed.

"Shit, after Optimus told me to drop her off at the bus station one night that she turned up at his apartment. She offered me some pussy, thinking I was gonna drive her home or something. I hit that shit and still dropped her off at the bus station."

He fell out laughing.

"Shit, she sucked my dick before that when she asked me to take her home before Op called you, Demon," Crew spoke up, and I couldn't help but laugh.

"It's all good, because my dick hasn't touched her in months."

I then turned my eyes back to Pussy Wap.

"My nigga, what did she tell you… that I was her nigga and mistreated her or some shit?" I asked, and he didn't respond, but from his face, I knew I had it right.

"She was never my girl… just a pussy to drill when I was bored, and when my queen came along, I didn't even look at her ass again. She's mad because I didn't want her ass, and she tried to kill my fucking girl. Look… now she sent you to die for her just to set me up, but she's been around me long enough to know that can't no fuck boy police lock my ass up!"

"She didn't set me up to die. She wouldn't do that," his dumb ass said. "Nigga, you ever heard of a nigga called Grim?"

I only asked because I knew there was no way this fool knew who the fuck I was and still tried this shit. I bet my ass that Goldie never told him who I really was.

"Yeah, I heard of him. Why?" "What you know about him?"

"That he's a killer and someone that nobody can fuck with," he said, proving my point.

"Nigga, what the fuck this say?"

I turned the gun to the side so that he could see my fucking name engraved on my shit.

"Deshaun motherfucking GRIM Jones, nigga!" I read out for him, and his eyes widened like saucers.

Chuckling again, I said, "Like I told you, the bitch sent you to die. Why else didn't she tell you my fucking name? Where the fuck she at?"

Goldie only got away from me at the hospital because I was injured and didn't have my guns, or I would have just shot the bitch right between her fucking eyes.

"She was at his house, but—"

"Let me guess… she left out this morning or some shit, right?" I cut off the young dude and asked, and he nodded.

"How convenient," I said sarcastically. She really thought that he would rob me successfully and get my money, or she was hoping I would get killed or go to jail for killing old dude. Either way, she wasn't expecting me to not get a hit one way or another.

"She would have disappeared by now, Grim," Demon said, and I agreed.

"I'll get her eventually when she realizes her plan never worked. She will resurface," I let him know.

"Nigga, next time… do a background check on pussy before you fuck and find out about the nigga you're trying to rob."

I laughed.

"Oh wait… there won't be a next time for you," I said before busting my guns on him. I nodded for my niggas to lay down the rest of his boys except the young nigga. He looked like a got damn baby, and I knew in my heart he was just following orders.

"What's your name, nigga?" I asked him, putting my guns away as Demon called Trevor to come and get these bodies. I wasn't worried about anyone seeing or hearing, because luckily for me, these lame niggas hung on an abandoned street. All the houses nearby were empty.

"Devon," he said while looking at me.
"Give me your wallet."

I outstretched my hand, and he handed it over. Crew searched him to see if he had any weapons on him, but he was clean. Looking through his wallet, I pulled out his ID and shook my head.

"Young nigga, you only eighteen fucking years old?" and he nodded yes.

"I ain't gone kill you as long as you never saw shit and you don't know shit, right?"

"What you talking about? I don't know a damn thing," he said, and I nodded my head.

"You talk, and I will find you. I have your ID, and by the time you get home... nigga, I will know who your mama is, where you went to school, your church... nigga, even what you ate today for breakfast. You understand what I'm saying to you?"

"Yeah, I heard about you, Grim. I know how you roll," he said.

"Glad we understand each other, Devon. Now, take yo' ass home to your mama, and keep off the fucking streets, or you gonna end up like your peoples here."

I pointed to the four dead bodies on the ground. Devon nodded his head and then took off running.

"You sure he won't talk?" Crew asked.

"Yeah. He's a good fucking kid. He was just tryna fit in on the streets.

Nigga has a fucking library card. He doesn't belong out here." I showed them the card.

"He was probably tryna get some money to stunt on bitches with."

I laughed, and they agreed. A few minutes later, Trevor

pulled up in his black van. He gave me a head nod before jumping out the van with three other niggas and getting to work. I handed him an envelope of money and left him to it.

"Let's go," I said to my boys, and we headed for the car.

"I still can't believe both of y'all messed with Goldie too."

I busted out laughing when we climbed into the car and drove away. "Man, she was whack too. I couldn't even feel her walls," Demon fussed. "That's because she was fucking with Optimus' pet dragon!" Crew yelled

out, and we cried laughing. I'm so glad I dodged a major bullet with Goldie. I could have never lived it down if I made her my wife! She had no self-respect or morals, and I wished like hell I had never ever fucked her to begin with. One thing I knew was that I couldn't wait to see her again. I was gonna kill her with my bare hands.

Forty-five minutes later, Crew dropped me off home. After thanking my boys, I went into my house through the garage to dispose of my clothes and sneakers. Crew was gonna get rid of the whip we rode in, because I knew some type of blood traces would have been left in it from our clothes. Once I was down to my boxer briefs and wife beater, I entered the house. As usual, the house smelled sweet from all the fragrances Kaliyah would be using to keep the house smelling fresh. I thought I would have hated it smelling all fruity and shit, but I didn't. It was a nice reminder that I had a woman of my own that I lived with.

I made my way to the kitchen, because I knew my baby cooked me something good to eat. When I found my plate in the microwave, I rubbed my hands together with a huge smile and warmed it up. She had made fried chicken, mash potatoes, corn on the cob, and gravy. As my food warmed up, I got a cold corona from the refrigerator. Once my food was hot to my liking, I sat at the table and scoffed that shit down in minutes. My baby could throw it down in the kitchen.

After washing my plate up, I took my satisfied ass to my bedroom to shower. When I walked into the room, I couldn't fight the smile that plastered on my face from the sight of Kaliyah. She was lying asleep on our bed, curled in a ball with her knees almost in her chest. The T-shirt she had on had ridden up, giving me a nice view of her panties and sexy little ass.

I quickly rushed to the bathroom to shower so that I could climb in bed with my girl. It took me ten minutes to clean myself, and I didn't even bother with clothes, because I was about to wake my baby up to some D. I loved sleepy sex with Kaliyah, because I was able to have my way with her being half awake. Don't get me wrong, she was up for pleasing me when she was awake, but sometimes, she liked to get on top to take control. She was more submissive when sleepy, and I loved giving her this D like that, because her ass would be crying out and begging me for mercy.

I climbed in behind her and pressed my body against hers as my hand ran over her booty. It only took a few seconds before she woke up, and like the good girl that she was, she instantly rolled over for me. That shit sent me crazy. She didn't fuss or complain when I woke her up for sex. She just rolled over and gave daddy some loving.

"Hi, babe."

She smiled and pushed her panties down for me.

"Hey, beautiful," I whispered to her, stroking her cheek. I

helped her out of her shirt and rolled on top of her. My hands squeezed every inch of her baby soft skin, and then she opened her legs and wrapped them around me.

"I love you, Kaliyah," I panted as I slid my dick deep into her, making her gasp.

"I love you too, Deshaun," she whimpered from my deep strokes. I continued to hit her with those death strokes until I got up on my knees and turned her on her side. With one of her legs on my shoulder and the other spread wide, I dug my dick deep into her.

"Mmmmm, yessss," she hissed. I licked my thumb and then brushed it against her clit. She bucked, and I chuckled when I saw her do that. I knew her nub was sensitive as shit.

"Ooooh, shit," I grumbled low in my throat. I grabbed her left breast that was bouncing around and squeezed. Dropping her leg that was on my shoulder, I leaned over and sucked on her breast.

"Ohhhh yes, Deshaun. Right there," she panted, and I sped up, knowing I was on her spot. Seconds later, whimpering in a low sexy voice, her cream coated my dick as she came.

"Let me get a hit of that," I said, pulling out of her, turning her on her back and licking her love box. I made sure to get it all before picking her up off the bed and slamming her down on my waiting dick.

"Fuck!" I yelled out when her pussy clenched and held me captive. With a firm grip around her waist, I bounced her up and down. She threw her head back, giving me access to suck and lick on her neck. I felt my nut rising from how good the pussy was feeling.

Nobody could tell me shit. I knew this girl was made for me. Her body fit so nicely in my arms. She lit up my soul just from me seeing her face. She calmed me in a way only my mama could, and her pussy fit my dick like a mold. This girl was my wife, and my whole body knew that shit!

"Cum again for me, baby," I whispered to her. Her eyes were closed tight, and her bottom lip was tucked neatly between her teeth. I smiled at her beautiful face all contorted from the beating my dick was giving her. I grabbed both of her ass cheeks. Spreading them slightly, I pounded away, making loud sounds as my dick beat against it.

"Uhhhhh," she cried and came again. "Good girl."

I smiled at her, and then I placed her down on the bed on all fours. She had hers. It was time to get mine.

She curved her back perfectly for me, giving me a good view of her fat pussy. Licking my lips, I climbed behind her and pushed myself back inside. She had a mini orgasm just from feeling me back inside. Giving her ass a nice little slap, I held her waist and rotated my hips slowly into her. She moaned and balled the comforter in her tiny fists.

"Deshaun."

"I love you, Kaliyah. I love you so damn much, baby," I mumbled as my body shook.

"I love you more," she managed to breath out before my ass went fucking crazy. I grabbed around her neck, firmly but gently, and pumped rapidly… deep and hard. After every few strokes, I would rotate my hips into her before going back to my assault.

"Shit!" she screamed.

"You're mine forever, Kaliyah. Do you hear me?" I

growled, sweat dripping from my face as well as trickling down her back.

"Ahhhhh shiiiitttt!"

I bucked and shook with my eyes rolling back in my mind. "Got damn!"

I let go just as I spilled my baby juice into her. Panting, we fell down onto the bed, and she rolled over to me, placing her head on my chest. If this was what love was all about, I was set for life! There was no place I would rather be and no one I would rather be with but her.

Looking down at my future, I smiled, because it was a beautiful sight.

We made love for hours until we both fell into a peaceful sleep.

Chapter Seventeen

Goldie Lawson

I KNEW I SHOULDN'T HAVE TOLD all that shit about Grim to Slim, but it was only because I needed a place to stay, and I thought he would have just felt sorry for me and allowed me to stay. I wasn't expecting the nigga to actually try and do something about it!

What started off as just a few lies here and there about Grim had turned into something completely different, and I didn't realize it until I heard him planning to rob Grim earlier in the day. I wanted to tell him not to do it, especially because I never told him that it was Grim. I kept referring him to my bitch ass ex, but when he started asking me questions about his name and where he hung out at, I only answered because I didn't want him to figure out that I had been lying. I told him my ex's name was De and left it at that.

I told him everything but his name, and that was because everybody knew about Grim, even though only a few people knew what he looked like. I was afraid that if he knew that Grim was the man I was talking about, he would have put me out or something.

Slim was a nigga that I had met at my cousin's party a year ago. I would fuck around with him whenever Grim disappeared on me with another bitch. He wasn't from Manhattan originally and had moved from Trinidad around the time I had met him. He was a street nigga where he came from, and he came here to get away from trouble that he had got into with the police out there.

His friends, who came from Trinidad with him, weren't keen on me, and they were forever telling him not to trust me. I wished I could have stopped him from going after Grim. It was just too late for that. If Grim surely didn't kill me, Slim would, and at that point, it was Slim or me! I already knew he didn't stand a chance against Grim, and I didn't need to stick around to find out.

It was a shame, because he did have a nice dick, and he ate my pussy, unlike Grim. Plus, he had a nice little set up going on just off Wall Street, and I knew Grim would have never found me there. After he tried to kill me in the fucking hospital like I wasn't shit, I knew I had to keep away from him. My plan to sneak into his room and kill him in his sleep had failed. I didn't expect the nigga to be awake that soon.

Mmmm, maybe Slim might kill him instead, I thought to myself as I made my way out of Manhattan. Don't ask me where the fuck I was going, because I had no idea. I just knew staying at Slim's condo wasn't an option. I didn't know whether or not he would tell Grim where I was. Slim wasn't a pussy, but he wasn't a nigga like Grim.

"Damn."

I shook my head. After everything that happened and how Grim easily choked the shit out of me in the hospital over that bitch, I still couldn't think about him without my pussy jumping. They just didn't make niggas like Grim anymore!

"This was all that bitch's fault!" I grumbled to myself. Everything was perfect before she came along. Now, I was in fear of my life because of her! He didn't even care that she was the one who stabbed him! Well, I made her do it, but she was the one who was holding the knife.

He really loved the skinny little young bitch! I wished I went back to that house and killed her perfect ass, but no. I just had to keep my ass at the hospital, hoping to win Grim's heart back, only for him to still pick her. I wasted all that time being up at the hospital every day, waiting for him to wake up when what I should have done was gone back to that house and killed the bitch. Then, he wouldn't have had a choice but to get with me. Now, I knew he had taken her to his house, so there was no way that I could kill her now… even if I did know where that damn house was.

My eyes burned as a few tears tried to fall over Grim. He gave her everything on a silver platter! I would never know how it felt to have him in the way that she did… to have him love me the way he loved her. I bet he even fucked her differently because he loved her ass. God knows what it would have been like to taste those beautiful thick lips of his. *Damn, imagine those shits on my pussy.*

I dragged my small suitcase behind me as I made my way to the bus station. I ended up leaving all my good shit at Grim's house and getting what I had left at my mama's. After I fled from the hospital and after hiding in the bushes from Optimus, I went straight to my mama's and got the rest of my stuff before I headed for Slim's. My mama asked me to come home, but I knew that I couldn't. Grim and his niggas knew where she stayed at. I wouldn't have lived to see the next day.

When I arrived at the bus station, I looked around at the departure information to find the next leaving bus. There were two about to leave within the next hour, but before I could make a choice of which one to take, I looked up and locked eyes with someone I wasn't expecting to see.

Oh my God! I hope he doesn't kill me!

Chapter Eighteen

Deshaun 'Grim' Jones

GOLDIE WAS DEFINITELY GONE. We looked everywhere for her, but no one had seen her since before I woke up in the hospital. I expected once her nigga was dead that she would try her hand again at some shit, but she was quiet as shit. We checked his apartment off Wall Street after getting his address from his ID, but she was already gone just like that young nigga, Devon, said.

It had been three weeks since I murked that nigga. I figured that she probably fed him some bullshit so that she could stay with him and didn't expect him to act on it. Who the hell sends someone after somebody but doesn't tell them who the fuck it is? He wasn't prepared at all for me. He was acting like I was some random small-time nigga that he could just fuck with. However, he still had to die. I didn't need that nigga to come back harder.

The streets were quiet once again, and things were all good. One of my niggas told me that Tuts got picked up by some traffickers. I guess that was some karma for her ass! She tried to sell Kaliyah like a prostitute and ended up getting the shit done to her instead. I didn't tell Kaliyah. She didn't need to know anything about that woman anymore. The only thing was… Tuts' words that night didn't sit right with me.

Why couldn't I be with Kaliyah? What did she mean by I didn't know who I was with? Something about how she said it made me nervous. Anyone who looked at Kaliyah could see that she was nothing like her mama, so I knew that wasn't what she meant… but what?

It was a little after 9 pm, and I was finally taking my black ass home. My dad had a new shipment come in, and I had to deal with that. It took me a few hours. Now, I could lie up under my girl and maybe sling some dick her way! I opened the door and was surprised to see that the kitchen light was on. I was expecting to find Kaliyah in bed with a movie or book. She lived a simple life, but I liked that shit.

"What's up, baby?"

I smiled when I walked in.

"Hey, babe," she said quickly with a smile, before going back to whatever she was looking for in the cabinets. She had a plate full of strawberries, a big glass of what looked like a strawberry smoothie and a jelly donut.

"What's up with all this strawberry stuff, baby? What are you looking for?"

I chuckled at her, because she looked like a crazy woman frantically searching.

"Do we have any peanut butter? I really want some," she said before pushing her head into another cabinet.

"Um… no. I don't eat that shit… and what the hell you gonna do with that? You don't even have anything for that to go with," I said as I pointed at her array of food.

"I was just gonna eat it with a spoon," she complained.

"Oh, shit!" I put a fist to my mouth and laughed.

"I done knocked yo' ass up, haven't I?"

Her eyes opened widely as she looked back at me.

"What?"

"I think I got you pregnant, babe. Ain't no other reason for you to want that shit to the point you look like you're about to cry."

I laughed, and her mouth dropped.

"But I can't be, Deshaun. I'm only eighteen! I don't know how to have a baby!"

"Well, are you on birth control, because I haven't been using any condoms?"

"No… but you haven't been releasing in me, Deshaun."

Shaking my head, I said, "Baby, I've been letting loose all in that pussy… multiple times too. That's my fault. I should have made sure you were on something."

When I saw her little ass start to panic, I walked over to her and pulled her into my arms.

"I know you're young, K, but I've got you, baby. I'm not gonna leave you on your own. I'm gonna be here every step of the way," I reassured her. I didn't imagine myself having any kids, to be honest… however, I liked the idea of Kaliyah walking around with a little me inside of her. Only thing now was that I think it was time for my parents to finally know about her!

I pulled back a little to look at her face. She looked up at me with fear and hope lining her big dark brown eyes. I meant every word that I had said to her. I wasn't going anywhere!

"Come on. Let's go to the store to get a pregnancy test and your greedy ass some nasty peanut butter," I said, and she smiled so wide I had to laugh. I couldn't believe she was happy about getting some damn peanut butter.

One hour later, and after making me buy not one but THREE jars of god awful peanut butter, we made it back home to find out that I did get my baby pregnant... Daddy Grim!

***

It was like as soon as we found out that Kaliyah was pregnant, the morning sickness hit her and started kicking her ass. I felt sorry for my baby. Everything smelt nasty to her, and she spent a lot of time vomiting. I had to change my cologne four times before we found one that didn't make her feel sick. She ate because she felt sick, and she felt sick because she ate, yet my baby didn't complain or cuss my ass out. She was taking it like a soldier, and a nigga was hella proud of her.

Now, I was outside of my parents' house, about to tell them about Kaliyah and my seed. I wasn't worried about my mama, because she was always telling me how she wanted me settled down, but my pops was another story.

I entered the house and went in search of them. They were both out in the garden since it was a nice warm day. My pops was fooling around with his latest toy boat, and my mama was laid out on a lounge chair while reading a magazine.

"Hey, mama... pops," I called out, and they both looked over at me. "Oh baby, I didn't know that you were coming here today."

My mama approached me and kissed my cheeks. Next, my pops pulled me in for a quick hug and gave me a head nod.

"Yeah, I um... I wanted to talk to y'all," I said. Damn, I

could go on a fucking mission and not feel a damn ounce of fear, yet having to tell my parents about Kaliyah made me feel like I was about to walk the plank or something.

"Sure, son. Let's go into the house. I need something to drink," my pops said, leading the way. I allowed my mama to go in before me, and I followed them into the living area. My pops offered me a drink, but I declined. When he got his drink of preference, he came and sat opposite me, next to my mama. They both looked at me and waited for me to start talking. I cleared my throat and thought, *shit… what's the worst that could happen?*

"I um… I came to tell y'all that I met someone," I said, and my mama grinned while my dad just rose an eyebrow at me. I went into the story about how we met but left out who her bitch ass mama was and what her uncle did to her. All they needed to know was that she was having problems at home, ran away, and I found her. I made sure to mention that me getting stabbed had nothing to do with her, even though it did. I didn't want them to think she tried to hurt me. As long as I knew the truth, that's all that mattered to me.

"Awww, Deshaun, does she make you happy?" she asked me.

"Yeah, she does," I answered her with my eyes on my pops who had yet to say a word after everything I had just said.

"Pops?"

His silence was making me nervous. He flashed his dark eyes up at me before looking over at my mama.

"Miriam, can I get a minute with our son alone, please?" he asked her. She looked down at him since he was still sitting on the couch while she and I were standing. She gave me a reassuring smile before doing what he asked and leaving the room, closing the door behind her.

"Son," he started with a shake of his head.

"What have I told you about these bitches out here!" he lowly complained.

"She's not a bitch, pops. She's a nice girl, and if you just met her, you would see that for yourself."

"I told you to fuck them, find one to give you your seeds to only, but not to love them... or damn sure not let one live with you!" he continued.

"Pops, I fell in love. I can't apologize for that," I said, and he looked at

me.

"What's the big deal anyway? You have always told me that, but you never told me why?"

"Because bitches are ungrateful, Grim! No matter what you do, they will still shit on your heart like you ain't shit!" he spat angrily. I was beginning to think that he was talking from experience, but he couldn't be talking about my mama like that... could he?

Huffing and puffing, he stood to his feet and walked over to me. There weren't any niggas alive who scared me, but my pops did, even though I knew he wouldn't hurt me. Other than that night he had to let me know that he was the king, he had never had to put his hands on me, and I damn sure didn't want him to. He was a big ol' nigga, and he would probably fuck around and kill my ass!

"Pops you know how much I respect you, and I do everything you ask me to do, but there is just something about her. I couldn't help falling in love with her, and that's why I've come here to let you know. I want y'all to at least meet her, pops. Can we at least start from there? Not all women are the same, pops. My mama is a good woman," I said, and hearing him scoff made me feel uneasy. My mama was the most beautiful person I knew, outside of Kaliyah. However, from my dad's reaction, I was beginning to think that he thought otherwise!

"Is she obedient?" he asked, and I snorted. "Pops, she's not my child or a dog."

"I know that shit, but will she listen to you if you tell her to do something?
That's what the fuck I meant."

"Yeah, pops. She trusts me and follows my lead," I answered honestly. At first, it did take her awhile to trust me, and since she has, no matter what I told her, she trusted a nigga.

"Okay, we can work with that. When a woman can be controlled, you won't get any problems with them," he said, and I looked at him.

"Problems like what, pops? I don't understand. She isn't a hoe like that. I know she won't step out on me," I let him know, but he just put his drink to his lips and took a sip. Without another word, he walked to the door, pulled it open, and told my mama to come back in.

"So, when are we going to meet this girl?" he said, surprising me, and I smiled with a shake of my head.

"How about y'all come over tomorrow for dinner."

"Can she cook? I'm not trying to get food poisoning," my dad said, and my mama sucked her teeth at him.

"My baby has skills, okay?" I said, and he nodded.

"Alright, we will be over tomorrow evening at six," my dad said, and I agreed. *Shit, at least he agreed!* Like I said before… what's the worst that could happen?

Chapter Nineteen

Kaliyah Diamond

"**D**AMN, K. I KNEW THE DICK WAS GOOD, but shit… I didn't know it was that good to get you caught up in the moment! Now your ass is pregnant, bitch!"

Pedra laughed as we sat in the kitchen. Today was the day that Deshaun's parents were coming over to meet me, and I was nervous as hell.

"Shut up, Pedra. I thought he was doing that *thing*," I said, referring to the pulling out method. I was new to this relationship thing, but I knew men did things like that. Zoe told me her ex-boyfriend did it all the time, and she never ended up pregnant, so I just imagined that's what Deshaun was doing. I didn't know how to ask him if he was.

"You're dick whipped!"

Pedra laughed at me, and I rolled my eyes at her.

"You ready to meet them?" she asked, and I shook my head no.

"Oh shit. Don't be nervous. His mama is nice. I've met her once on Optimus' birthday one year. She's a beautiful little lady. She was nice to me, and I ain't shit to Deshaun. I already know that she's gonna like you."

She smiled at me.

"But his pops…" she let out, and I popped my eyes out. "Why? What is his dad like?"

"I've never met him, but I heard he's a hard nigga to get along with. Just imagine Grim… but taller, thicker, bald, with a long ass beard, and evil as fuck… and that's his daddy."

She gave me a look that I didn't like.

"Pedra, shut the hell up! You with your damn stories always scaring me! You told me that Deshaun would shoot me for accidentally stabbing him and made me go on the run. I was scared for my life!" I said, and she laughed.

"Bitch, you're the one who fell in love with a nigga named GRIM!"

I waved her off and continued with my finishing touches around the kitchen. I had out all the drinks that he said his dad liked to drink, and I had fresh juice for his mama.

"What did you make to eat?" Pedra asked, walking around and trying to have a look in the oven.

"Baked salmon, yellow rice with collard greens, and a peach cobbler for dessert."

Smiling, I was happy with what I had made. "Oooh, bitch, that's it. Impress the parents!" She danced, and I pushed her.

"You need to go now. They will be here in about thirty minutes," I said while pulling her toward the front door.

"Shit, I get the message. Call me later, boo."

She gave me an air kiss and walked out of the door. I waved at her as she disappeared down the street before closing the door and running around to make sure the house was perfect. I was scared shitless, even though Deshaun told me that I had nothing to worry about.

"His dad couldn't be that bad," I whispered to myself,

thinking about what Pedra had said. That girl was crazy as they came, and she was always making things sound worse than they were.

I sat in the den, staring into space until I heard the keys in the door.

"Shit," I mumbled, and after fixing my maxi dress, I slowly headed toward the door. Deshaun walked through first, and when he saw me standing in the hallway, he gave me a lovely warm smile.

"Hey, baby. You are looking pretty as hell."

He walked toward me and gave me a quick kiss on the lips. He stroked my hair and winked at me, making me blush.

"Where are your parents?" I asked, because they hadn't walked through the door as of yet.

"Oh, they decided on bringing some gifts for you. They're just getting them out of the car," he said, rubbing on my ass.

"Let me see if they need any help."

Giving me a quick kiss, he rushed back out of the door. He was so excited, and it was cute to see him like that. I knew this was a big moment for him.

I blew out a nervous breath and rubbed my sweaty palms down the front of my blue dress before running a hand through my hair, making sure it was fine. I literally held my breath when I heard footsteps coming toward the opened door.

A huge shadow appeared before a giant man who looked just like Deshaun walked through the door. He was so tall that he almost hit the top of the door frame. Next, a beautiful, shorter lady walked in and stood in front the tall man, and Deshaun stood beside her.

"Mama… pops… this is Kaliyah," Deshaun said with a huge smile on his face that instantly dropped when he caught sight of his parents' faces, and they didn't look very happy to see me!

****

Deshaun 'Grim' Jones

I COULDN'T UNDERSTAND WHY MY PARENTS were just standing there, staring at Kaliyah the way that they were. My mama had tears in her eyes, but my daddy looked mad!

"Mama?" I called to her as she took a step toward Kaliyah. "Pattison, look!"

My mama pointed at Kaliyah who was standing there looking scared out of her mind.

"Mama, what's going on?" I called out to her, but she was looking up at my dad as tears flowed down her cheeks. My pops took one look at her, and next thing I knew, he charged over to Kaliyah and pulled her by the hair. Screaming, I ran over to him and jumped on him as he pulled Kaliyah down to the ground.

"POPS, PLEASE LET HER GO!" I begged him. Kaliyah was screaming, and that shit was hurting my heart like a motherfucker.

"Pattison!" my mama screamed, pulling on his arm trying to get him off Kaliyah. My dad was a big nigga, so even with me and my mama pulling on him, he wouldn't budge. He dragged Kaliyah across the floor, still holding her hair.

"POPS, SHE'S FUCKING PREGNANT!" I hollered at him, and he stopped to look at me. I never told them about the pregnancy yesterday, because Kaliyah and I wanted to do it together in person. He looked down at Kaliyah without loosening his grip, and then my heart started beating out of my chest when he pulled his gun from his waist.

"POPS, NOOOOOOO!"

I jumped on his back.

"Pattison, please don't! I'm begging you, please!" my mama begged with a wet face.

With my mama pushing herself between him and Kaliyah, I was able to wrestle him away from Kaliyah who was crying hysterically at this point.

"Pops, stop! Calm down, please," I begged him as he tussled around the room with me still holding him. I looked over at Kaliyah, and I wished that I could get to her, but my dad still had his gun drawn, and God knows I was afraid to let him go.

"Kaliyah, let's go!" my mama yelled out and pulled her up off the ground. My dad raised his gun, and I grabbed that hand. Thankfully, my mama ran out of the house with Kaliyah just as my dad threw me to the ground and chased after them.

What the fuck was going on????

****

Kaliyah Diamond

"RUN, KALIYAH!" MRS. JONES screamed as she pulled me toward her car. My head felt like it was on fire from how hard Mr. Jones had been pulling on my hair, and my knees were burning from being dragged on the carpet. I looked behind me, and when I saw Mr. Jones running out after us, I let out a frightened scream. Mrs. Jones opened her car, and we climbed in just as a gunshot rang out behind us.

"Ahhhhhh," I screamed and ducked down in the seat as Mrs. Jones pushed her foot on the pedal. We went flying away from the house.

"DESHAUN! HE'S GONNA KILL HIM!" I panicked.

"He won't hurt his son, Kaliyah!" she shouted out without looking at me. I looked over at her, and I couldn't help the tears that fell from my eyes. When I woke up this morning knowing I was going to meet his parents, I didn't expect it to end like that. I didn't understand what I had done and why his dad wanted to kill me.

Mrs. Jones continued to drive like a bat out of hell, but she didn't say another word to me. I didn't know where we were going, if Deshaun was really okay, or what the hell was going on?

"Mrs. Jones, I don't understand. What did I do? Why did your husband just try to kill me?"

"Kaliyah, where have you been?" she asked, ignoring my question.

"What do you mean? I've been in Harlem with my mama. Do you know me or something, because I only met you today?" I questioned.

What did she mean by where have I been? Had she been looking for me? Did she know me? How did she know me?

"Mrs. Jones?"

"Kaliyah, I've known you since you were born," she finally answered, and then she grabbed her purse and emptied its contents on her lap. Continuously switching her view from the road to her lap, she threw things to the ground until she found two folded photographs that she handed to me. Shaking, I took the photos from her, and my eyes damn near fell out of my head when I looked at the first picture.

"That's me, you, and your daddy," she said. It was a picture of her standing next to a man that I looked remarkably so much alike, and he was holding me. I couldn't have been much older than one in the picture.

"You knew my daddy?" I finally found my voice and asked.

"Ohhh, he was my best friend. I loved him so much. When he died, I looked for you baby. I swear that I did. Where were you, Kaliyah?"

"I lived off West 125th Street with my mama."

"And who's your mama? He never told me. After your mama got pregnant with you, he wanted to keep you both safe, so no one knew who she was, and he died before he told me."

She looked over at me.

"My mama, is Tuts," I admitted.

"TUTS? Oh my God. You were right under my nose. After

looking for years, we all thought you were dead," she said, and although she was explaining things to me, I still didn't understand anything.

"How did my daddy die?"

"He was killed. None of us knew by who, but judging by how Pattison just reacted to you, I now know it was him… this whole time!"

She punched the steering wheel.

"Mr. Jones killed my daddy?"

Chapter Twenty

Deshaun 'Grim' Jones

I RAN OUT AFTER MY DAD just as I saw my mama screech away from my house.

My dad even shot after them, but it didn't hit.

"Pops, what the fuck was that? I knew you weren't happy about me falling in love, but did you really have to try to kill her! I don't understand that shit!" I yelled to his back. He suddenly turned to face me and grabbed me by the throat.

"How the fuck did you end up with her?" He squeezed my neck, choking me.

"I told you… I found her when she ran away from home," I croaked, and he let me go. He stomped off into my house, and then I heard shit breaking.

"Fuck," I breathed and went in after him. In a few seconds, he managed to fuck up all the shit in my living area, including my got damn TV.

"Pops! What the fuck, man?"

"YOU FELL IN LOVE WITH THE SEED OF MY ENEMY!" he yelled, and my mouth dropped.

"What… what are you talking about?"

"That little bitch is the seed of Lester Johnson!" he roared.

"Lester Johnson? Who the fuck is Lester Johnson, and how the hell was I supposed to know that shit when she doesn't even know who her dad was?"

"If you weren't too busy falling your pussy ass in love and leaving seeds behind, none of that shit would have mattered! Yo' mama... I knew she still loved that nigga!"

He punched a hole into my wall.

"Mama? What do you mean?" I asked, but he didn't answer me.

"I killed a nigga for her, and she still betrayed me for him," he mumbled to himself.

"Pops!" I called out, and he swung around to look at me.

"Grim, I have another job for you... I want you to kill Kaliyah, your mama, and that bastard seed, or I'm gonna kill you!"

Chapter Twenty – One

Kaliyah Diamond

"BEFORE HE DIED, YOUR DADDY kept saying that someone was after him, but he didn't know who. He was getting threats and all kinds of things were happening around him. At first, I thought that maybe he was paranoid, but then, his car was blown up… and his house.

He didn't want anyone to know where you were or who your mama was, because he didn't know if they would kill you too. He planned on taking you and letting his parents raise you, but he was suddenly killed before he could. Only a few of us knew about you, and I looked for you for years. I searched, but I never found you. Then, we were told that you were killed, and I stopped looking for you. There was no record for a Kaliyah Johnson—"

"My name isn't Johnson… it's Diamond," I corrected her.

"Diamond? Well, where the hell did that name come from, because your mama's name is Pettigrew," she said.

"What? She told me that our last

name was Diamond." I was even

more confused now.

"That's probably why I couldn't find you. I searched for your name and date of birth but found nothing from after you were born. I remember that night you were born. Your daddy was so happy."

She smiled.

"Kaliyah, your daddy loved you more than life. You must

know that."

I looked down at the photo with him again, and a few tears fell from my eyes. I didn't remember him, but it was nice to know that he loved me. The way he was looking down at me in the photo with the biggest smile on his face, I knew it was true. After looking at it for a few more minutes, I remembered that I had another photo that I hadn't looked at yet.

"Is this…?" I asked when I unfolded it and looked at it. "Yep, that's you and Deshaun."

She smiled from ear to ear. I laughed at the picture. Deshaun must have been about four years old, holding me in his arms with a huge smile on his face. He looked so happy holding me.

"The two of you have been destined from the beginning. I made a pact with your daddy when you were born that you would marry my son."

She chuckled, and I laughed, but our laughter was short lived when we remembered what we were fleeing from.

"Mr. Jones wants me dead, doesn't he?" I asked with more tears building behind my eyes.

"Yes," she answered, and I

nodded my head. "Why?"

"Because now everyone will know the truth that he was the one who killed Lester, and because you being alive will change a lot of things. Pattison doesn't want that, so he won't stop until you are dead… and probably me too," she said, and I sat quietly.

I was in love and pregnant by a man whose father wanted me dead. I looked down at the picture with baby Deshaun, and I prayed that he was okay, even though I now knew that whatever we had was over.

Sometime later, Mrs. Jones stopped the car. I looked around and recognized that we were in Harlem, but I wasn't sure where.

"Here... put this cap on. Keep your head down, and don't look at anyone, okay?" she said, and I nodded my head. I pushed my hair underneath and pulled the cap down low to hide my face.

"Follow me, and remember to keep your head down. It's imperative that no one sees you. All it will take is one look, and they will know without a doubt that you are Lester's daughter," she said. I didn't say a word. I just kept my head down and followed her into some kind of lounge.

The place was full of men and women drinking and smoking. That smoke made me cough a little, and I felt a pain in my side when I did, but I just ignored it. Mrs. Jones pulled me by the hand and headed into the back of the establishment without saying a single word to anyone. When she came to a big brown door, she pushed it open without knocking.

"Miriam? What are you doing here? I'm not trying to get my ass beat by Pattison. You know that nigga don't really like me already. He thinks I want you," a voice called out to her.

"Django, that's not important right now. I need you to shut down right now, and call the others. This is not a joke, Django. Some real shit is about to pop off. We need to go underground right now before Pat gets here," she rumbled off.

"Shit... what's going on, Miriam? Is Pat coming here to kill me?" the man asked.

"No... me," she said, and then it went quiet. I couldn't see the man, because I was standing behind her, and my head was down like Mrs. Jones had told me.

"You know the code, right?" he asked, and Mrs. Jones said that she did.

"Give me an hour, and I will meet you out there. Be careful, Miriam," he warned before she turned to face me and pulled me out of the building.

We climbed into a different car, and she sped off. Thirty minutes later, we pulled up at an abandoned looking factory. Mrs. Jones entered a code at the gates and drove in when it opened. She drove to the end of the path before stopping the car and climbing out. I followed behind her as I looked around at this place. It looked like it had been years since anybody had been out here. I was surprised the gate and code still worked.

She led me to a huge metal door and entered another code. The door unlocked, and after taking a look around, she stepped inside.

The inside didn't match the outside, because it was done up nicely like someone lived there. It was a large room that reminded me of a bomb shelter or panic room that people built in the basements of their houses. Mrs. Jones told me to take a seat on the couch and handed me a bottle of water from the cooler.

"How far pregnant are you?" she asked.

"Four weeks," I replied after gulping down a mouthful. "Who could imagine me with a grandchild?"

She chuckled.

"Oh, you look so much like him," she said to me as a few tears fell from her eyes. We sat in silence for what seemed like forever until hearing the door open. I jumped to my feet. In walked a few men that I had never seen before.

"Okay, Miriam... what's going on? Why did we need to

come out here, and why is Pattison after you?" this man who looked like Jamie Foxx said to Mrs. Jones. Without saying a word, Mrs. Jones pulled me to my feet and pulled off my cap. The men instantly glued their eyes on me, and a look of shock covered all their faces.

"But... but how? Kaliyah? You're alive?" the man asked me, approaching me.

"Damn, you look like yo' daddy." He chuckled with tears in his eyes.

"I'm your godfather. Your daddy was my cousin," he said, smiling. "I'm Melvin Johnson, but people call me Django."

He shook my hand.

"How did you find her?" he turned to Mrs. Jones and asked. "I didn't. Deshaun did," she said, and he looked back at me.

"Okay, and why is Pat after you, Miriam. I don't understand," another man asked.

"Because he was the one who killed Lester," she said, and the men gasped.

"Miriam, you can't accuse someone of something like that... especially not Pattison. Lester loved that man like a damn brother. We all did," the man said again.

"Okay, well you explain why he saw the seed of his supposed friend and tried to shoot her!" Miriam said, and they looked at me and then her.

"When?" Django asked.

"Just before I came to you, Django. Deshaun and Kaliyah are together, and we went to their house to meet her for the first time. As soon as I saw her, I knew who she was, and I expected Pattison to be happy like I was, but he pulled his gun out. That let me know that he was the one who killed Lester," she explained.

"But why? That doesn't make any sense," another man called out. "Yes, it does," Django said and dropped down on the couch.

"Fargo was getting ready to step down, and he wanted someone to replace him. Pattison was sure that it was going to be him, but he picked Lester. Lester was supposed to be the new king once Fargo stepped down. I saw how Pattison changed toward Lester after it was known who Fargo chose, but I just thought he was just jealous and that it would pass," Django said as he shook his head.

"After Lester was killed, I felt like it was Pattison, but I didn't want to believe it. We were boys... closer than blood! I couldn't believe that Pat would kill our brother like that. Even when Pat took over from Fargo, I chose to forget about it all."

Everyone in the room looked around at each other, and then their eyes landed on me.

"You all know what is going to happen, don't you?" Mrs. Jones asked, and they all nodded.

"Pat is coming for her," Django said, pointing at me. "And he's not coming alone."

Chapter Twenty – Two

Miriam Jones

"OH, LESTER… HOW COULD PAT do that to you?" I spoke to myself as tears slid down my face. Kaliyah and I were hiding in Lester's safe place that he set up for himself but never got to use. Only Django and I knew about this place, so I knew that Pat wouldn't easily find us, however, I knew that he wouldn't stop until he did.

"I found her, Lester. I finally found her. Forgive me for stopping and believing she was dead. None of this would have happened if I had found her earlier. Now that I have found her, I may lose her again, but I promise I will die first before I let anyone kill her."

More tears poured out. I thought that my eyes would never see Kaliyah again. I remembered holding her as a little baby… the cutest little girl I had ever seen. She was the carbon copy of her dad, and just from the little time I had spent with her, I was already in love.

I would admit that I was in love with Lester and had been since I was sixteen years old when I first saw him around the way. He was the most beautiful thing I had ever laid eyes on. His dark silky hair and boyish features did something to me every single time I saw him. He was a street nigga, and I knew that he was, but he had a certain shyness about him that I loved.

His weird friend, Pattison, always had a thing for me and would always try and talk to me whenever he was alone, but I couldn't help the way I felt about Lester.

I used to lay in my bed at night and dream about being with him almost every night. My parents, who were Christians, knew that I liked him, and they were not very pleased about it. They were forever telling me to find a nice little church boy, but I didn't want that. I wanted Lester. He used to make my soul feel like it caught on fire from the way he used to look at me. No one had ever made me feel the way that he did. I was hopeful that one day he would come for me, and we would live happily ever after.

That was until Pattison told me that Lester liked a girl I went to school with. My heart was broken! I tried not to believe it until the day I saw them out together. That was the day I made a terrible mistake and gave in to Pattison's advances. He was a handsome young man, and there were enough women around that were into him. I was surprised that he still wanted me after all the time I had turned him down for Lester. The only reason I decided to give in was because I told myself that I would rather spend my time on a man who did like me.

Pattison was good to me, but I noticed his and Lester's friendship changed slightly, and I didn't find out why until Lester came and told me how he felt about me. I was crushed! He told me that he didn't approach me sooner because I was only sixteen at the time and was too young for him, but as soon as I turned eighteen, he made his feelings known.

By then, I was pregnant with Deshaun. I was furious at Pattison for lying to me, but I couldn't put all the blame on him. I should have been woman enough to ask Lester.

My parents were angry that I was pregnant and forced Pattison to marry me. I went along with it for my son's sake. I wanted him to have a good life and have a chance to know my parents who were threatening to disown me if I didn't get married.

I knew it hurt Lester to see me marry Pattison and have a child with him, but we decided that we would become best friends instead. Although my heart never ever stopped loving him in that capacity, I was grateful to still have him in my life. We were almost inseparable. If he wasn't on the streets, he was with me. Pattison wasn't too pleased about it, but he accepted it. We spent all our time together until Kaliyah came along.

The way Deshaun looked at her the first time was how I used to look at Lester, and I knew at that point, as young as he was, he was in love at first sight. The few times that we spent with her, he did everything in his power to make her happy and protected her. If a toy hurt her, he would hit it for her. It was adorable.

"You know they're gonna get married when they get older! If they don't, something is wrong!" Lester used to always say, and I would laugh. We made a stupid pact one day that he would save his daughter for Deshaun.

The four of us were happy, and we spent almost every day together until Lester started telling me that someone was after him. He stopped seeing Kaliyah for a few days in case someone would follow him to her.

He was sure that he wanted to get her some place safe. He thought that people not knowing who the mother was wasn't safe enough for her. I wasn't angry when he wouldn't tell me who she was, because I knew the life he lived and that it was only to protect her.

He did, however, tell me that he was going to bring me to meet the mother and his parents so that if he was killed before he had a chance to take her, I would do it for him. At first, I thought maybe he was being a little paranoid until he left my apartment and I never saw him again.

I remembered crying for days and days. Not only did I lose my best friend, but I lost Kaliyah too because I had no idea how to find her. No one knew who did it, and his crew combed the streets looking for answers… answers that never came.

It didn't even cross my mind that Pattison could have been the one to do it. Yes, their relationship had changed, but it changed on Pat's part, not Lester.

Lester still loved him as a brother and trusted him. He just thought Pat believed he would try and take me from him, and Lester never thought of doing that.

When he decided to be my friend, that's all he ever saw me as and wanted from me. I was the one who kept that love for him in my heart, and that wasn't anything he did. I never told him, so there was no reason for Pat to feel some type of way toward Lester.

Despite that, no one suspected Pat. I would have never known until he tried to kill Kaliyah in front of me. I begged and pleaded for her life. Seeing her was like I had a part of Lester again, and not only that, but I made a promise to him the last time I saw him, that I would look after his daughter once he was gone.

God knows that I looked for her everywhere, but there was no record of her. I had no idea her mother changed her name but now that I thought about it, I would have done the same. I'm sure Lester would have expressed his concerns to her, and then he ended up dead, I would have changed Kaliyah's name too to protect her.

She was a fucked-up person for the things she did to Kaliyah. That's why Kaliyah ended up running away, but she did the best thing by changing her name. Pat would have found her and killed her without a doubt.

When Deshaun told us what she went through before he

found her, my heart broke after finding out he was talking about Lester's Kaliyah. I knew she wouldn't have gone through any of that had I had found her.

Life for us now was bad. I knew Pattison, and he wouldn't rest until both of us were dead. I didn't care about me. I had lived my life. My only concern was Kaliyah's. My mind was already made up, I would sacrifice myself for her to get away. Hopefully, she would be able to. Django felt the same way, and I knew that with both of us, she had a better chance at getting away.

My only regret except for not finding her first was that she and Deshaun would never get to live the life that Lester and I wanted for them. Pattison had a hold over Deshaun in a way that I knew he would make him choose between his own life and mine. Although I didn't want my son to have to kill me, I would rather it be me than him, and I was at peace for that. I just wished that Kaliyah could live.

Every time that I said to Deshaun that I wished he would settle down and have a family of his own, I was talking about Kaliyah. Both Lester and I invested some money into an account that Django kept after he died. That money was to ensure that both of them would be happy and have a life away from all of this. I tried my hardest to keep Pattison from turning Deshaun into his own personal slave, but whatever Pat wanted him to do, he did.

I knew without a doubt if Lester survived, Deshaun would have never known the street life. That's one thing Lester promised me… that he would never accept Shaun on his team, but none of that mattered now! Soon and very soon, Deshaun would find us. I just hoped it was later rather than sooner!

Chapter Twenty – Three

Pattison Jones

SEEING KALIYAH WAS LIKE I was staring into the face of Lester again. She looked like he literally spat her ass out. I wasn't expecting to ever see her, because I thought I had killed her! No, I was sure that I did, so how was it that she was still alive? Not just that, how the fuck did she end up with my son?

A part of me felt like this had to be some type of sick joke or a nightmare, because it couldn't be real. I also believed that somehow, Miriam set it up for Grim to find that little bastard seed. Of ALL the women in New York, my son just had to find her! That shit didn't make sense to me.

I wasn't a nigga who was afraid of shit, but I'll admit… when I saw her face, fear took over. It was like Lester was having the last laugh from the grave. No one but God knew that I was the one to kill Lester, and I wanted it to stay that way. It was crucial that no one knew. Now, I knew I had let that information out by trying to kill Kaliyah in front of Miriam, but fuck it! I couldn't stand there and look at her face. I could hear Lester taunting me as I stared at his face that was on her.

Miriam… she broke a nigga down when I saw the way she was looking at Kaliyah. From the tears in her eyes, I knew it was more about Lester than Kaliyah. It was like she had a piece of him right before her. She didn't even care to hide the shit from me! I wished I never loved her the way that I did and that I'd had the courage to kill her years ago.

Since that nigga died, something in Miriam changed, and she was never the same again. I killed that nigga for her, and she just wouldn't stop loving him! I thought I won when I got with her first, but I had her body, and he had her heart.

For as long as I could remember, Lester had a thing for Miriam, but he never made a move, because she was young at the time, and he was a street nigga. He didn't think she would want anything to do with him, knowing that. I too had been looking at Miriam.

I was cocky enough to believe that in a choice, she would have chosen me, but she didn't. She loved that nigga too.

That was the start of my bitterness and jealousy for my brother. I went behind his back and told Miriam that he was after one of her friends, and she believed me. I didn't give her a chance to find out the truth before I made my move. My mind told me she allowed me to fuck because she was hurt by Lester supposedly wanting her friend instead, but my pride wouldn't let me believe it. By the time Lester grew enough balls to finally tell Miriam how he felt about her, I had gotten her ass pregnant with Grim. Miriam was hurt that I had lied to her, but she stayed with a nigga.

I know now that was because of the principle of things and not because she actually wanted to be with me. I knew that Miriam wouldn't have gone there with Lester after being with me. She wasn't a female like that. She believed that a woman should never fuck two friends.

I thought I had finally won, but the two became close regardless and chose to be best friends instead. They shared everything and were always together. It shouldn't have bothered me, however, it did! Every time she looked at him, I saw love in her eyes… a love that she didn't have for me. Her parents made her marry me because she had my son, and that was the only reason.

Even they didn't like me for her. I should have walked away at that point, but I loved her! I knew that every time he saw me, it hurt knowing that I was with the woman he loved.

I was happy to know I had one up on him, but that was short lived when Fargo picked that nigga to take over for him. His reason was because I was too unpredictable. He stepped over me and picked Lester. Seeing everyone showing him the respect that was meant for me and seeing my wife in love with him led me to kill that nigga.

At first, I was just sending death threats to him, hoping that he would walk away from the streets and leave it to me. However, that nigga had more of a spine than I had thought, and he stayed, even after I blew up his fucking car and house. People actually started admiring him more, and it was like every time I turned around, his name was coming out of somebody's mouth, including Miriam's!

I knew then that he would have to die. I was supposed to find out who the fuck his baby mama was and kill that bitch too with her baby, but circumstances caused me to jump the gun, and I shot that nigga when we were alone together in the warehouse. I took his body to the river and burned his remains. Then, I shot myself and made it out that we were ambushed and had gotten separated.

Everyone believed me because of how close I used to be with Lester. He was my brother, and I loved him, but I loved myself more. I deserved to be with Miriam and be the king, so I took it! The only problem I had left was his seed. He never told me or Miriam who the mother was, leaving me no idea where she was. I didn't know until a bitch texted his phone a week after I had killed him. She asked him for some diapers, and I figured she was the baby mama.

I got her address from tracking her cell number. I snuck into her house in the middle of the night and killed her with her baby that I assumed was Lester's seed. For seventeen years, I believed I got away with it, and that everything to do with that nigga was dead. Here I was, looking at my failure. I killed that nigga to win my wife's heart and the streets, and now, all that shit was in vain.

Word soon started to spread that I was the one to kill Lester, and just as I foresaw, the streets divided in two with more niggas taking up for Lester. I was slowly losing my damn streets!

"Grim!" I yelled out to my son from my den. I hadn't slept or eaten since I came face to face with Kaliyah. All I had been doing was sitting, thinking, drinking, and smoking.

"Yes, Pops," he answered as he walked into the room.

"What the fuck is going on? Haven't you found them yet?" I grilled him. This wasn't his doing, but I expected him to have found them before the news got out about her.

"Not yet, pops. Shit is mad right about now. I can't even walk down the street without niggas shooting at me!" he complained.

"DON'T YOU THINK I FUCKING KNOW? LOOK WHAT THE FUCK IS HAPPENING TO MY STREETS! EVERYTHING IS IN FUCKING CHAOS."

He looked at me but didn't say a word.

"Look at the fuckeries your mama and girl are doing! It's a fucking war zone. You should have gotten at them before this shit happened!"

I looked at my son, and it was taking a lot of strength not to knock his ass out. I knew he was procrastinating because of who they were, but he was my only solution. No one could track niggas down like my son.

"Deshaun, I know this isn't an easy task, but you are my son. I wanted you, and if your mama could have had it her way, you wouldn't even be here. She wanted to abort you, and I fought to keep you," I said, trying to appeal to him.

That shit wasn't true. His mama loved him from the moment she found out that she was pregnant with him. However, he didn't need to know that. I needed him to hate his mother and get the job done.

"You just remember that, son. Now Kaliyah, she is her father's child, Grim. She will end up destroying your life. Believe me, son. You didn't know her father. I did. She has the same spirit. You don't need her. You just need me! There's plenty more women out there for you."

I walked toward him and put a hand on his shoulder. Looking him in the eyes, I said, "These are our streets son. We put in all the hard work. Seventeen years I have run the streets, and now we are close to losing it. Is that what you want?"

"No, pops."

"Good, son. Good. All you have to do is get at your mama and Kaliyah, and everything will go back to normal. It will be just you and me."

I laid it on thick. He locked eyes with me and nodded.

"You need to find them now, Grim. No more time… do you hear me?"

"Yeah, pops. I hear you."

"Let's show the streets why I'm the king and you are the prince."

I smiled, and he nodded his head. I wasn't going to give the streets up without a fight, and if it was a war that they wanted, then it was a war that they were going to get.

After all, I had killed for the streets before, and I would do it all over again… wife or not!

Chapter Twenty - Four

Deshaun 'Grim' Jones

"**S**HIT!" I HOLLERED AND BUSTED MY GUN. One of Lester's men snuck up on me at the fucking gas station, and I had to lay him down in broad daylight. I didn't even get the chance to pump any gas before he was up on me. I couldn't even stop to get some once I shot him. I hightailed it out of dodge.

"Fuck!"

I punched my dashboard a few times. Things were as fucked up as they were going to get. This war was ridiculous. They were adamant to protect Kaliyah and my mama. Niggas my pops broke bread with were rolling up at our spot and shooting at us. All the traps were hit and burned down to the ground.

My boys were missing in action, but I already knew what was up with them. Their pops were hardcore Lester riders, and I knew they had switched sides too. That was the most fucked up part. Before, I had everyone in my corner, but now, I had enemies because of my pops. All this shit was before my fucking time. I didn't even know this Lester nigga, yet I was the one who had to deal with the aftermath.

I heard what my pops said, but something didn't add the fuck up. How could you take out someone you called your brother for the streets? I didn't understand that shit.

By the looks of things, my pops would have done well with that nigga by his side. But one thing I knew about my pops, he didn't do partnerships. He took it all!

After checking my mirrors to make sure no one was following me, I pulled my phone out. I needed to call my pops.

"Pops, you need to call your detective friends. I had to lay a nigga out at the gas station," I said once he finally answered.

"Where, and who the fuck you killed like that?" he asked with an attitude.

"Pop, you're acting like I had a fucking choice. The nigga just rolled up on me in broad fucking daylight. It was him or me!"

These niggas were getting reckless. Most of our fighting was done at night where there was fewer witnesses and shit. This was the first time I had to kill someone in front of people since this whole shit started.

"Who the fuck was it?"

"Freddie," I said, and my pops went silent. I knew Freddie was considered a loyal soldier, but his loyalty was with Lester.

"Fuck! It's like all my best niggas are on the other side. SHIT!" my pop yelled into the phone. He wasn't lying there. Other than me, my pops didn't really have anyone like that. Most of the men who sided with us were newbies who didn't even know this cat, Lester, but all the long serving true soldiers like Django and his crew were now fighting against us.

Don't get me wrong. We still had some niggas who were nice with guns and their hands, but shit… they didn't make niggas with spines like the OGs.

"Grim—" my pops called me, and I already knew what he was going to say.

"I know, pops. I know!"

"This shit should have been done yesterday," he lectured me. He thought that it was easy for me to just fucking hunt my mother and girl like they were dogs. I knew that shit needed to be done. It just didn't make the shit easier!

Everyone who knew me knew that I was a motherfucking mother's boy! I didn't give a fuck. That woman was my heartbeat, and then I met Kaliyah who also took up residency in my heart. I never loved someone the way that I loved her. Now, I had to kill the only two women that I had ever loved. The unfortunate thing was that it was either me and my pops or them. One pair had to go. That much I knew.

"Grim, you told me you got this. You said you understood what needed to be done. Do I need to take over, because I will? I'm trusting you to deal with this shit, but let me know if you can't, and I will deal with it."

"Pops, of course you can fucking trust me! When have I ever given you a reason not to?"

"You haven't, but there's a first time for everything!"

His words silenced me. Was he really questioning my loyalty like that? "Pops, I got this. I'm gonna end this soon," I finally answered.

"That's what I like to hear. Meet me at the warehouse. I've got something that may be able to help."

We discussed meeting up and ended the call. There was no more avoiding the inevitable. I had to shut shit down and now. Like I said, it was either them or us, and I wasn't ready to die just yet.

All I could do was ask God for forgiveness!

Chapter Twenty – Five

Kaliyah JOHNSON

TO FIND OUT THAT MY FATHER WAS KILLED by Deshaun's father was a mind- blowing thing. It hurt me to know that they all grew up as brothers, but Mr. Jones allowed jealousy to lead him to kill my father. From the stories that everyone told me about him, my father was a good man... a street man but a good man. He spent every single day with me up until he was killed. Django even had a few more pictures of my dad that he gave to me.

I had grandparents out there somewhere, but no one knew them or their names to even try and find them. My dad kept his family life separate from the streets, and he kept his parents away from it so that if anything did happen, they wouldn't get hurt in the process. That's why he planned on making me go to live with them, as a sure way that I wouldn't be found.

This bomb shelter type place became my new home with Mrs. Jones. We were not allowed to leave out of fear of being found by Mr. Jones and Deshaun. I knew when Django said that Mr. Jones was coming for me and not alone that he was talking about Deshaun. I knew what he did for his dad. I just never ever thought that I would become a job!

Maybe it was for the best, because a day after getting here, I suffered a miscarriage. I knew it was due to the events that led me to this place that I had been in for almost a week. It was a difficult thing for me to go through, but Mrs. Jones was good and helped me through it. I missed Deshaun so much, but I knew in a choice between me and his father, his father would win.

Now, I found myself surrounded by men who were willing to die for me off the strength of my dad. I was catapulted into a world that I knew nothing about and wanted nothing to do with it, however, it was my destiny from the moment I entered the world… I was a street king's daughter!

There was even money left for me by my dad. Django never touched the money in my dad's account in hopes that they would find me. I now had more money than I could count, yet I was a prisoner in this world. Oh, and I was being hunted by the man I loved.

The life I left behind with my mama didn't seem so bad anymore. Here I was waiting to be found and killed. It was a frightening thing to be hunted.

Optimus, Demon, Goliath, and another man who called himself Chicken were now amongst the men who I found posted around me. I was worried and surprised to see them, but I was told that they, along with their fathers, were loyal to my dad. Once the truth came out about Mr. Jones being the one to have killed him, the streets erupted into a war with half the people following Mr. Jones and half following me, even though I had no idea who I was leading and to where. Surely, this was some kind of mistake or nightmare!

These men looked to me to take over for my dad, but, how could I? I didn't know a got damn thing about any street life. I knew enough from the time I spent with Deshaun and the things he used to tell me, but living it was a completely different thing. I had even asked Django to take over, but as Lester Johnson's only child, that mantle, unfortunately, fell in my lap. Because I had no husband, I was the only option.

Django told me that I didn't need to worry too much about

the empire. He would explain everything to me in due time. I guess this situation with Deshaun and his dad took precedence over me being the so called street queen... ME... little old me, who, other than running away from home, had never spent a day out on the streets. Granted, I was no longer that fragile little girl who people walked over, I wouldn't say that I was street enough to run a damn drug empire.

Since I suffered my miscarriage, I had locked myself up in my room, or should I say a storage cupboard that was made into a bedroom. Mrs. Jones kept checking on me and giving me food, but I just needed some time to myself. I didn't know how long we would be here or how long it would be until Deshaun eventually found us. All I knew was that I was on borrowed time!

****

At some point, I had drifted off to sleep after sitting alone on my bed deep in thought. That was suddenly interrupted when I heard a lot of commotion outside of my room. I slowly crept off my bed and opened my door.

Everyone seemed to be on high alert with people shouting out orders, rushing around the room. They were so busy with whatever was going on that no one noticed I had come into the room. Mrs. Jones was standing by the door with Django discussing something as Optimus, Demon, and Goliath stood loading up some big ass guns.

"What's going on?"

The room fell silent, and everyone had their eyes on me. Django and Mrs.

Jones looked at each other before they both approached me. "He's found us," Django said with a hand on my shoulder. "Who found us?"

"Deshaun... he's outside," Mrs. Jones said. I looked around the room again, and seeing everyone looking like they were about to step into a war made my heart race.

"But why do we need all these guns? Are you going to kill him? You can't kill him!"

"Kaliyah! He is not here to talk. He is here to kill you and possibly as many of us as he can. Do you think I want to kill my only son? But, if he comes in here, I will have no choice. He will not stop until you are dead... and me too," Mrs. Jones said with tears in his eyes.

"His father sent him for both of us, and he will do it without hesitating whether I'm his mama or not. Do you understand?"

She shook me. This couldn't be happening! Before I could respond, a loud boom shook the room. Chicken and Demon opened the door and rushed out. Goliath and Optimus locked it behind them, standing guard at the door.

A few people had been killed since this whole thing started, including the older men who were here on the first night, so there were not many of us in here. I had heard stories about Deshaun, and I already knew that the seven of us were nothing for him!

My whole entire body was frozen with fear as I stood trying to see if I could hear any sounds outside. I gasped when I heard a gunshot and looked over at Mrs. Jones. Either Deshaun shooting one of the men, or it was them shooting Deshaun. I didn't know which one I preferred. I didn't want to die, but I didn't want Deshaun to die either.

Boom! Boom! Boom!

The sound of someone pounding the door echoed in the room that was now deathly silent.

"Open this fucking door, or I will kill them! NOW!" Deshaun's voice roared through the steel door.

"I'm not gonna ask motherfucking twice!"

Everyone looked at each other, but no one said a word back. Optimus peeked through the blinds and then turned to face us.

"Chicken is shot, and he's got a gun to Demon's head," he whispered to us.

"How the fuck did he find us?" Django asked, and everyone shrugged their shoulders.

"Open the door," I said, and everyone looked at me like I was crazy.

"Kaliyah, he will kill you," Django said, and I looked at Mrs. Jones. I wasn't ready to die, but if that was my destiny, then it was what it was.

"I don't want anyone else to die for me," I sniffled because tears had started to pour out of my eyes rapidly.

"If I'm going to die, then so be it. Open the door," I said again, and Mrs. Jones nodded her head yes. I guess we were both at peace. As soon as the door opened, I wiped the tears from my eyes, straightened my back, and held my head up high.

All my life, I had run away, cowered, accepted abuse, and cried, but if today was going to be my last day on earth, I wasn't going out as the old Kaliyah. I would do it with my head up and not a single tear in my eyes.

Deshaun stepped over the threshold with an arm around Demon's throat and a gun to his head. Using a foot, he kicked Chicken into the room who was holding onto his arm that was bleeding profusely. Another man that I didn't know walked in behind Deshaun with two guns drawn.

I looked Deshaun in the eyes, and I made sure not to show any fear, even though I could just die from how scared I felt.

"Back the fuck up!" Deshaun growled to Optimus and Goliath. They slowly backed up with their guns still drawn. Deshaun then looked over at me, and his face was emotionless like he didn't know who I was.

"How did you find us?" Mrs. Jones called out, and Deshaun looked over at her before his eyes fell on me again.

"I see you're still wearing the chain I gave you," he said to me with a smirk on his face, and his friend started laughing. *Oh my God! Did he put a tracking device in the chain he gave me?* I looked down at it and then back up at him.

Almost like he could read my mind, he said, "I sure did, baby."

I felt the blood in my body run cold. *Did he always know that one day he would have to kill me? Why else would he put a tracking device in my chain?* My mind was riddled with thoughts as I stared into space.

"DJANGO! Don't move, nigga! Now, you of all people know I'm not wrapped too tightly, my nigga," Deshaun called out.

"Oh, this is going to be so much fun!" he said, kicking the door closed behind him and releasing the hold he had on Demon who he then pushed over toward us. I looked up into the eyes of the man I loved as he raised his gun and then... *POP!*

To be continued... Nah just playing!

Chapter Twenty – Six

Deshaun 'Grim' Jones

IT HAD BEEN THREE DAYS SINCE I DID the unthinkable, and it was killing a nigga. My decision kept fucking with me and eating my ass alive, but there was no turning back. It was done! I had to lay low afterwards, but I mainly spent the time trying to get my mind right, because a nigga felt like I was about to lose it!

"Pops!" I yelled out as I searched his house for him. I had not seen or spoken to him since that day, and I needed to fill him in. I knew he must have been blowing up my phone that I turned off, but shit… that wasn't some easy shit that I did. A nigga needed a minute!

It felt weird walking into the house and not hearing or seeing my mama… or not smelling the sweet aroma of her cooking. I made it my mission not to come to this house since everything kicked off.

"Pops!" I continued until finally, I heard the front door open and close. I guess he really wasn't in the house.

"Grim!" he yelled, and I sighed out. "I'm in the kitchen, pop."

A few seconds later, his large image appeared in the doorway.

"Why the fuck have I been looking for your ass for three fucking days!" was the first thing he said when he saw me.

"Pop, you know I always lay low after a job."
"But I wasn't expecting you to do that this time 'round. I was

expecting for you to come to me first! Why the fuck you needed to lay low for three days anyway?" he quizzed with an angry look on his face.

"Because I didn't know if anyone saw my ass going into that fucking building. You already know the streets are in chaos. There are still some of Lester's niggas out there. I couldn't take any chances," I said, and he nodded.

"So, what the fuck happened? Did you kill them?"

I turned to look at him, and I felt ashamed but angry that I was forced into this situation to begin with.

"Yeah, it's done," I said, and the way he was smiling sent shivers down my spine.

"Well, where's my proof?"

Looking at him like he was crazy or something, I asked, "What proof? You never asked for any, and I never give any. You always taught me that no proof and no witnesses meant no evidence."

I did what I had to do, but he was fucking crazy if he thought that I wanted a reminder of that shit!

"Okay, what did you do?"

"I shot everybody and set that shit on fire." He nodded his head with a smirk.

"How did you find them though, Grim, because I looked every-fucking- where? Why the fuck didn't you call me?"

"Pop, there was no time for that. I was told a location, and I had to roll with it just in case they got away. Freddie told me right before I shot that nigga. He thought by telling me I would spare him," I lied, and he nodded.

Shit, he didn't need to know that I had given Kaliyah a chain with a tracker in it. He would have gone off on me, and a nigga needed time to process the fact that I needed to kill my own fucking mother and woman! There wasn't any rushing in that shit, so I took my fucking time.

"How many of them were there?" he threw question after question at me.

"Seven of them."

"Wow… your mama was something else," he shook his head.

"Anyway, where the fuck is Lex?" he asked about that nigga I had with me.

"I told him to lay low too. Nigga is probably somewhere balls deep in some pussy."

I chuckled, and he nodded with a smile. Looking me in the eyes, he asked, "So you good, son? How do you feel after killing your girl and baby?"

"Shit, she was just a bitch like you said… plenty more where she came from."

I half smiled, and he chuckled.

"And yo' mama?" he asked. I couldn't even talk, but I knew I had to say something.

"I just closed my eyes and pulled the trigger," I said.

"Hmmm," he hummed rubbing on his chin. Next thing I

knew, he backhanded me across my face, making me fall to the ground.

"DO YOU THINK I'M STUPID?" he roared, walking toward me. "You and your mama both squint yo' eyes when y'all are lying!"

He grabbed me up off the floor and started choking me. I tried to get his hands from around my throat, but he was too strong. My body shook as he sent powerful blows to my face, stomach, and ribs before dropping me to the ground. I coughed and spat out blood. My ribs felt like they were on fire.

"You think I don't know you didn't kill those bitches! I know you didn't… with your pussy whipped and mama's boy ass. Plus, I told Lex to hit me up as soon as you killed them, and I haven't heard from that nigga, so I know you killed him."

He bent down to my level and spoke in my face.

"You wanna know how else I know you're lying?" he asked, but I didn't answer him.

"Because you're still breathing, nigga. I told Lex to take you out as soon as you killed those bitches. I didn't need your mama's boy ass to come for me in the middle of the night or something," he said, and my jaw dropped.

Yeah, I didn't kill my mama or Kaliyah. I loved them too fucking much.

Let's go back for a minute…

"Oh, this is going to be so much fun!" I said with a smile on my face as I kicked the door closed. I raised my gun and sent one shot into Lex's head, making everyone jump. I dropped my

gun and rushed to my mama and Kaliyah, pulling them both into my arms. I don't remember the last time I cried, but I let the flood gates open as I stood with them in my arms.

"I could never hurt y'all, but I needed Pop to believe I would or he would have killed y'all himself. I wish I could have come to y'all earlier. I wanted to, but Pop wouldn't leave my side. Then, he sent this nigga with me," I explained as I rained kisses on both of their faces. I knew that I had scared them, but I would rather die than to kill them. Kaliyah trembled in my arms as I professed over and over again how much I loved her.

"My bad for shooting you, my nigga," I called over to Chicken who looked pissed the fuck off that he was bleeding.

"I had no choice. That nigga wanted to put a hot one in your head I had to think fast," he said, and Chicken sucked his teeth.

"Nigga, I don't care that you shot me! I'm mad because this is my fucking favorite shirt!" he bitched, and I laughed. I looked back at my mama and Kaliyah and held them in my arms for what felt like hours.

"Tie his bitch ass up!"

My dad's yelling cut my thoughts short. I looked up to see Crew standing in the doorway. He walked over to me, yoked me up, and pushed me onto a chair that he started tying me to. I spent the last three days comforting my mama and Kaliyah before we came up with a plan to take my pops out. As long as he was alive, he wouldn't stop until they were dead.

It fucked me up to have to make that decision, but now that I was here and he told me he asked Lex to kill me, I no longer felt bad. I was just pissed that now I would have to take out my cousin too. I guess that's why he wasn't answering my calls before… too busy being my daddy's bitch.

"I can't believe you thought I was that stupid, Grim. I taught you better than that, son. You and your mama think that I don't notice shit, but I do! I just play like I don't for you two fools! Like she didn't think I noticed all those years that she cried over that bitch ass nigga, Lester. Every fucking birthday and anniversary to his death, she moped around the fucking house like a ghost. Even in his grave, that nigga was fucking up my life, and now, his damn seed has corrupted my son!"

He punched me in the jaw, causing blood to well up in my mouth that I spat out on his floor.

"Look at my fucking empire because of that bitch and yo' mama… yo' mama! After everything I did for that bitch, she goes against me and helps to start a fucking war!"

"Don't talk about my mama or my girl like that, nigga!" I yelled at him, causing him to laugh at me like I was playing.

"I need those bitches, dead!"

He kicked at the chair I was sitting on.

"Daddy, didn't I tell you he couldn't be trusted?" I heard and looked in the doorway to see Goldie! Damn, that bitch came like roaches.

"Damn, pop… you left a queen and picked up a hoe. You do know that I smashed her as well as Optimus, Demon, and Darius, right?" I laughed.

"Shit, even Crew got his dick sucked by her!"

I continued to laugh, and her face dropped. My pops looked over at her like fire was coming out of his eyes.

"You told me that you only fucked my son!" he yelled at her.

"Daddy, he's just trying to cause problems, but he can't be trusted. Look… he lied about killing his mama and that bitch. I told you not to trust him. He's just mad that I don't want to be with him anymore," she whispered seductively to him.

"Bitch, you and I were never together! Fuck you! You were a pussy to fuck, and when I didn't fuck, I nutted on your face when you gave me head. You really believe I would treat someone I'm in a relationship with like that?" I yelled at her, and I could see the tears threatening to fall, but I couldn't give a fuck!

"You know what it was, Grim. Stop lying," she barefaced lied, and I shook my head at her.

"I'm over the mistakes I made being with you, Grim."

"And what about sucking my dick, Goldie?" Crew spoke up, and I laughed.

"I was high," she lied, and I snorted. "Yeah, okay," Crew answered.

"We are gonna talk about that later, but didn't I tell you to wait in the car?" my pops asked her, and she kissed his lips.

"Eeewww, pop! Not even I kissed the bitch in her mouth. You don't know where it's been. Shit, didn't I just kill yo' nigga, Pussy Wap, or whatever the fuck his name was? Skinny nigga with a fucked up eye?" I said, and Crew busted out laughing.

"Shut the fuck up! Yo' ass shouldn't be saying shit but telling me where the fuck yo' mama is," my pops yelled out to me. He called Crew over to him, and the two started whispering shit to each other. Goldie fixed her eyes on me, and then she came over.

"I loved you so much, Grim, and you shitted on my heart for that young bitch… even gave her a fucking baby, nigga!" she mumbled to me so that my pop wouldn't hear. Her saying that reminded me about my loss. I almost lost my fucking cool when Kaliyah told me she lost our baby, but I wasn't about to let that bitch know that. I wanted her to die believing I was about to have a family with Kaliyah.

"I should have pushed that knife in deeper."

She smiled as I looked at her, wondering what the fuck she was talking about.

"Oh yeah… it was me who made Kaliyah stab you. I pulled her hand toward your stomach, and you still chose her when you thought it was her! It's okay though. I'm gonna slice that bitch open once my man finds out where they're hiding. I'm not even mad anymore, because why have a prince when I can have a king instead?"

She laughed at herself.

"And he's so much better in bed."

"When I get out of this, you will be the first person to die. I promise you that, bitch!" I snarled, and then I started smiling real hard as I imagined finally killing that bitch. She didn't like what I said because the laughing she was doing only seconds before had abruptly stopped, and she had a look of fear in her eyes. I winked at her, and she backed up away from me.

"Oh, and you think I'm jealous over a nigga that's fucking behind all those other niggas? Demon said he didn't even use a rubber with you. He can have that waste land you call a pussy."

I laughed, and her mouth fell open before she walked out of my face and went over to my pops.

"It's okay. By the end of the day, this nigga will tell me what I want to know," my pops said to Crew before walking over to me.

"And after I kill them, I'm gonna kill you, nigga." He pointed at me with a laugh.

"Now is your chance, son, to show me what you're made of," he said.

"Fuck you, nigga. I ain't telling you shit! Fuck you, and fuck your empire! You ain't getting shit out of me!" I growled.

POW!

He punched me in the mouth again, and I wished my hands weren't tied up so that I could punch that nigga back. I had never had the balls to fight my pops before, but as of right now, he was no longer my pops.

"Keep your mouth shut, nigga, I wasn't talking to you!" he said, and I looked at him like *nigga what?*

"Oh shit, my bad. Have you met your brother, Crew?" he said to me, laughing, and I looked up at Crew. I always thought that he looked a lot like me in the face, but shit... I put that down to our pops being brothers.

"Hold the fuck up! You had a baby with your own brother's wife?"

"Hell fucking yeah!" my pops said like that shit was okay. Crew looked at me, and I guess he was just learning this shit too.

"Your mama was in love with Lester, and he was with her, but I told her that he was fucking around with another bitch because I wanted her so badly. By the time, they found out how they felt about each other, I fucked around and got her pregnant with you."

He pointed at me.

"However, after that, she was determined she didn't want any more kids and got her fucking shit tied without telling me."

I could see the anger in his eyes like he was talking about something that just happened and not something that happened over twenty years ago!

"I knew from the day you were born that I wanted you as my personal hit man, but I also knew in that line of work, you could easily lose your life too, and I needed a son who would eventually take my crown. I resorted to doing what I had to do, and Crew came along. As far as everyone knows, my brother is his dad, but I know he's mine. I had him tested when he was born."

I saw a look in Crew's eyes that let me know that he wasn't happy at what he was hearing.

"But now, since you've crossed me, Grim, I need your brother to step up and be my prince," he said to me, pointing at Crew.

"Take his ass to the warehouse. I will get what I need out of him there," he told Crew.

"Fuck, you!" I spat and then coughed when Crew punched me in my stomach. He leaned over and taunted me by whispering shit in my ears. That only fueled my anger. One way or another, I was getting out of this, and Grim was coming out to play.

Don't worry. I had a plan!

Chapter Twenty – Seven

Goldie Lawson

SEEING GRIM DIDN'T GIVE ME the satisfaction that I thought it would have. I wanted him to hurt seeing me with his pops like I was hurting seeing him with Kaliyah. However, he couldn't give a fuck and found it funny that his dad was with me.

The constant belittlement from him and name calling hurt me even though I tried my hardest not to show it. I was trying to get under his skin, but when he said that I would die first, I saw his eyes, and he was serious.

How did I end up with Pattison? He was the one I saw when I was trying to leave Manhattan after Grim killed Slim. He was at the bus station dropping off his latest play thing that came in from Texas. She wasn't anything to look at compared to me. At first, I was sure that he would kill me since I was almost sure that Grim would have told him that he was after me, but surprisingly, he offered to take me somewhere.

I told him how Grim found another woman and put me out like I was trash and how that woman had stabbed him. I told him that hoping he wouldn't accept Kaliyah once he did meet her, because he had told me that he hadn't yet and didn't even know that Grim was with someone like that. I used that shit to my advantage. I told him to take me to a hotel that he paid for, and we fucked for the first time.

Since then, I'd been sitting on his dick and whispering in his ear. I made his son out to be a damn liar, and I was just thankful that Grim fucked up by not killing his mama or that bitch, because it made Pattison believe everything else I had been telling him.

However, all my hard work may have been for nothing, because Grim just had to open his mouth about me fucking with his niggas and Crew! I was so surprised that nigga told that I sucked his dick. Truth be told, it wasn't Demon I wanted. It was Crew.

He looked so much like Grim and even had his mannerisms, so I went to Optimus' apartment, pretending I wanted to see him after hearing Crew's voice in the background when I called. I was still mad about Grim allowing Kaliyah to move in with us, and I thought that Crew was the perfect nigga to make me get over him.

Optimus was tripping about me turning up at his apartment, and said he was calling Demon to drop me back since I purposely didn't drive so that I could leave with Crew! I thought I would entice him to leave with me by sucking his dick. When he got up to go to the bathroom, I followed and did my thing.

Afterwards, he just nutted on my face and laughed at me when I suggested that we leave together. I was so angry that when Demon showed up to take me home, I rushed out of the house with him.

I needed something to make me feel better, and so I fucked Demon in the car. He didn't have a rubber, and I should have known better, letting him fuck me raw. I only did it because I was mad about Grim spending time with Kaliyah and then Crew rejecting me. A rubber didn't seem that important anymore.

After that night, I pretended like it never happened, and I wasn't expecting those men to have told Grim! I damn sure wasn't expecting him to announce that shit in front of Pattison. I only told him about Grim because that's all he needed to know. Now, I knew he was looking at me sideways.

No matter what, it was like Grim was always winning! How could he talk about me like that? He made it sound like my pussy was no good, but it had to be. Pattison said I felt fucking good after we fucked. Granted, his dick didn't fill me up like it should have, however, I put that down to his dick not being as big as Grim's. I mean, my pussy couldn't be that slack like Grim insinuated, right?

I was regretting getting out of the car after Pattison told me not to let Grim see me. I just wanted to parade me being with his pops in his face, hoping that it would hurt his soul like he'd done to me a thousand times. He killed my existence when I heard that Kaliyah was pregnant with his seed! That nigga fucked me with two condoms but gave her his dick raw! I hated her, and I hated him!

"Baby, did you hear Grim threaten to kill me?" I asked Pattison when he climbed into his SUV. I couldn't take the way Grim stared at me like he was threatening me with his eyes, so I hightailed it out of there and went back to the car. That's where I should have stayed in the first place.

I watched in the side view mirror as Crew dragged Grim and pushed him into the back of the SUV.

"Oh, don't worry about that," Pattison said nonchalantly like it was nothing, and at that point, I knew that what Grim had said had got to him. If I had never regretted something before in my life, I regretted the moment I went with Pattison. I should have just left and got as far away from this family as I could. I was too focused on hurting Grim back by getting with his dad, and now, here I was stuck.

I looked up into the rear view mirror and locked eyes with Grim's cold and dark ones. He gave me a look that made the hairs on the back of my neck stand up.

What the fuck did I get myself into?

Chapter Twenty – Eight

Deshaun 'Grim' Jones

I WASN'T A COCKY NIGGA. Well… most of the time I wasn't, but my daddy didn't raise no damn fool, and he should have known better! He really believed I didn't know that he asked that lame ass nigga, Lex, to kill me. Lesson 101, if you receive a fucking text from someone telling you to kill a person… DELETE THAT SHIT!

After I met up with my pops at the warehouse, he introduced me to this nigga, Lex. He told me how he wanted Lex to help me track down my mama and take her out. From the moment, I set my eyes on that nigga, I didn't like him, and I'm glad I followed my first mind. Something told me that he and my pops were in some type of secret plan, and as soon as I saw that text, I knew my suspicions were right.

Why the fuck would that nigga leave such a message on his phone knowing that he was gonna be around me? I didn't understand that shit. My pops, like a damn fool, texted Lex to take me out once I killed my mama and Kaliyah. He didn't outright say that shit. He used code, but he forgot that it was the same fucking code he would send to me when he wanted me to take someone out.

Lex was so fucking stupid. I knew he was hiding something from the way I would catch him looking at me. I knew that nigga wasn't gay, so the only thing was that he was up to something. Then, the fool left his phone and went into the shower, making it too fucking easy for me. Now, I knew only bitches snooped in nigga's shit like that, but fuck all that.

I didn't know this nigga from anywhere, and I wasn't in the

habit of just trusting niggas I didn't know. Of course, my black ass went through his shit. I needed to know who the fuck I was around, and I found my answer.

I knew from the beginning that I wasn't going to kill my babies, but shit, no one but me needed to know that. I also knew that it was either them or my pops. Seeing that he made the first move to get at me, it made it so much easier for me to put my plan in motion. Now, this stupid motherfucker was leading me right to where I wanted to go! Like I said, your boy had a plan!

Goldie sat up front, and she kept looking at me in the rear view mirror. From her eyes, I knew she was scared, but she was a dead bitch walking when she went into Kaliyah's room with that fucking knife. Fucking my dad didn't add to that shit. It just made finding her all that easier. I couldn't care less what she did with her whack pussy. The bitch was fucking foul, and I was embarrassed that I had ever stuck my dick in a walking disease cumbucket like her. She really believed she had shit on Kaliyah... *dumb bitch!*

Finally, we arrived at the warehouse. See, my pops kept a few secrets, like this warehouse for one. I knew he had it, but I had no idea where it was. He wouldn't allow me to it for some strange reason. I also knew that whatever crew members he had left were going to be here which was why it was imperative that I got here. If y'all could see the slick smile I had on my face, you would know I was about to be up to no good!

Stopping the car, my pops turned to look at me, and I dropped my head like I was afraid. I didn't need him to see the cocky ass smile on my face, because he would know I was up to something and probably would murk me where I sat. I needed to get inside for my plan to work.

"Take this nigga inside," my pops said to Crew who immediately pushed his door open and yanked me out.

"Do you have to be so damn rough, BRO?"

I put emphasis on the bro part. Shaking me roughly, he leaned over to me and told me to shut the fuck up before punching me in my stomach.

"Ahhhh, nigga," I choked, laughing at him.

"I see you," I added as he pulled me inside. Just like I knew, the last of my pops' crew were all inside. There were at least fifteen of them, and as soon as they saw me, they stopped what they were doing to stare at me. Crew pulled me over to a chair, pushed me to sit in it, and started to tie my arms behind my back.

"Could you at least fix my fucking pants for me? I ain't trying to get raped by one of these pussy ass niggas in here," I chuckled, being funny. I always wore my shit a little loose on the waist, and since my hands had been tied up for a minute, I wasn't able to pull those shits up myself. Huffing and puffing like some female, Crew grabbed the back of my pants and pulled them up as I stood as far as I could with my hands tied behind me.

"Whoa! Watch your hand, nigga," I told him, and he sucked his teeth at me.

"I'm not gay, bro. Plus, I heard my dick was bigger than yours," he said, and it was my turn to suck my teeth.

"Nah, no one could ever tell you that, my nigga. I've seen the bitches you fucked, and none of them had a limp. Didn't you see how Kaliyah was walking that last time you saw her?" I asked, and he mushed me in the head.

"I can't wait for you to fucking die," he said as he walked

away from me. My pops walked in with Goldie in tow. She looked scared shitless, walking behind him like a little ass girl. Well, I thought it was fear until a few of my pops' crew started calling out her name. Once a hoe, always a fucking hoe! By the way my pops looked at her, I knew that if he could., he would shoot her his

damn self. All he did was shake his head at her and make her come and sit by me.

"I didn't know you liked fucking the aged. You're supposed to help them, not suck them off!" I teased her.

"Fuck you, Grim. I wasn't a hoe like that until I started fucking with you. I tried to mask seeing you with other bitches," she said, and that shit made me laugh.

"Yeah… sure, Goldie… minus the fact you sucked my dick and let me fuck you outside in the parking lot of a club while your man waited in the club, holding yo' drink. Then, you kissed that nigga in his mouth after, knowing you just finished tasting my shit, but you weren't a hoe before that," I said and expected a response, but I never got one.

Looking around the room, I made a note of which niggas were close to me that I could easily take out. It was almost time, and I needed to get my plan of movement together.

My pops walked over to me with three men. One stood behind me, one to my left, and the other to my right with my pop stopping in front of me. All of them had guns out and held them down at their sides.

"Where the fuck is yo' mama, boy?" he snarled at me. I kept my head down and didn't answer him.

"ANSWER ME!" he roared, but I kept my mouth shut.

Delivering a fierce punch to my jaw, I looked up at him.

"You can look at me like that all you want to, but your mama caused this by loving that nigga. I didn't!" he said, and I dropped my head again.

"Keep an eye on him, and if he moves, shoot his ass in the leg or something, but don't kill him. Leave his ass for me," he said and walked over to another set of men. I looked up to see what he was doing, and as I did, I caught sight of the thing I was waiting for the most. With a smile that turned into a chuckle, I yelled out, "Pops... you wanna know where mama is?"

Turning to face me, he mean mugged me.

"She's right here, nigga!" I yelled just as the door blew open, and my niggas rushed in, guns blazing. That was my cue to start fucking some shit up! Pulling my hands out of the restraints, I pulled a gun from the back of my pants and shot the nigga behind me in the head. I then quickly took out the nigga on my right as Crew killed the nigga to my left while he ran toward me.

Yep! He was his brother's motherfucking keeper!

He had untied my shit when he kept punching me in the stomach, and when I asked him to pull up my pants, he pushed his gun down my back instead.

Hell was breaking loose around me, but my eyes were zoned in on one thing... Goldie! She was cowering behind a chair, screaming out her fucking lungs. With Crew covering me and laying niggas down, I ran over to that bitch and yoked her ass up.

"Grim! I'm sorry! I'm sorry! I will leave you alone from now on. I promise!" she pleaded with tears. She could plead all she wanted to. I was fucking done with her. No one was hurting my girl and getting away with it, especially as I had warned the bitch more than once. I wrapped one hand around her neck and put one on her head, holding her in place.

"Grim, please!" she begged one last time. "Bye, bitch!"

I snapped her fucking neck, letting her body drop at my feet with her eyes wide open.

"Ahhhh," I yelled out when a fucking bullet blew the top of my fucking left ear off. I looked up to see my pop's punk ass friend, Bernie, aiming his gun at me. Before I could shoot his ass, a bullet ripped through his head, and his body slumped. When I looked, it was Kaliyah! Yep, my baby had bossed the fuck up! I spent the three fucking days teaching her ass to shoot. Damn, if she was gonna be a street queen, she needed to know how to lay niggas out. She gave me a smile that made my dick rock up before looking around for who next to shoot!

I looked around for my mama, and she was standing by Django with Goliath shielding her and now Kaliyah who had walked over to them. My pops was busy ducking and busting his guns as his niggas dropped like fucking flies. I always made sure my boys were mean shooters like me, so this lame ass crew my pops had was shit compared to them. As soon as his last nigga dropped, he stopped shooting.

A few of my niggas got laid out, including Chicken, but I was happy to see that Django, Demon, Goliath and Optimus made it. Chicken was a soldier, and I would make sure his family was well taken care of.

Clapping and laughing, my pops came from behind the pillar he was using to shield himself. He walked to the middle of the warehouse as we followed. Looking around at all the bodies, he shook his head when he saw Goldie.

"I guess you were one step ahead of me, huh?" he asked me, and I smirked at him.

"Come on now, pops. You should have known you raised a thinker… or maybe I got that from my mama."

I laughed and blew a kiss at her.

"Why, Pattison? Lester loved you like a brother," she yelled out to him.

"I hated that nigga! You think I didn't know that you loved him? I saw the way you would look at him, and then when Fargo told me that he was going to make Lester the new king instead of me, I knew that nigga had to go. There was no way I was going to stand around and watch him walk away with my bitch and my streets. Fuck that nigga!" he said and spat on the floor. Kaliyah's face distorted, and I knew that action offended her the most.

"So, what now? You think this little ass girl can run the streets better than me? All of you, niggas ate because of me!"

He thumped his chest like a gorilla.

"Pattison, we lived like captives because of you. Those weren't even your streets to start with!" Django said, and everyone agreed. My pops had been bullying his way to the top like he did with James, and people were tired!

"Can't no bitch run these streets," he said, laughing.

"I don't need to! That's what my husband is for!" Kaliyah answered with a smile, and I walked over to her.

"That's right, baby," I said, planting a kiss on her lips.

Oh… my bad, y'all. Didn't I tell you that Kaliyah and I got married during those three days? My queen needed a king!

"So, you're the new king, are you, Grim?" he asked in a sarcastic tone. I looked over at him.

"Good for you, son."

He laughed and clapped.

"I guess I can't trust any of my fucking sons, huh?" he said, looking at Crew. Both my mama and Kaliyah looked over at me with questionable looks, but I told them I would explain it all later.

"Nigga, fuck you, and kiss my ass! Grim treated my ass like his brother from the beginning even when we didn't even know that we were. He was the one who gave me a fucking job, put money in my pockets, and watched my fucking back while you hid me until you wanted some shit from me!" Crew yelled at him. I knew he was hurt by what my pops had done.

"Man, fuck all of y'all! Now… which one of y'all think you're tough enough to take me out? I promise you I'm not an easy nigga to kill!" he said, sounding cocky as fuck. I looked down at Kaliyah and kissed her lips again. I handed Optimus my gun and took off Kaliyah's necklace, putting it back around her neck. That's how I led my people to the warehouse.

I pulled my tee and wife beater off before turning to face my pops.

Everyone made a circle around us as he pulled his shirt off. "You wanna fight me, young blood?" he mocked me.

"Hell yeah! You put a fucking hit on my mama and my wife. My seed died because you roughed up my baby when she was pregnant. Of course, I want that ass," I said, pacing in a boxer style stance with my paws up. I would be lying if I didn't say that my ass was scared shitless at the thought of fighting the man who birthed me and taught me everything that I knew… not to mention that he was a big old nigga, and his punches had the potential to fuck my ass up, but I needed to do this shit for my seed.

Catching me by surprise, my pops rushed me, and we went crushing to the ground. He landed on top of me, and he wasted no time putting in work to my face and head. In doing so, he left his side unprotected, and I knew he had fractured his rib in a bike accident a few years ago. Using that to my advantage, I punched him in his rib, and it winded him, allowing me to get up. My eye was trying to close, and my lip was busted, but I wasn't about to back down. This nigga had tried to take my family away from me and took my child. Fuck that. He wasn't my pops because he had no qualms asking a nigga to kill me!

We stood up and went round for round, blow for blow. I was happy to see that my hits were hurting him right back, but my body was burning all over from his blows. One thing he didn't have was stamina, and it showed when he started to slow his hits down. I was able to dodge a few of his punches and deliver my own because of that. He must have sensed that he was about to lose, because without warning, this nigga grabbed me into a chokehold.

"No!" Kaliyah yelled out and tried to come over to help me, but my mama pulled her back.

"No, he needs to do this, Kaliyah. This man had a hold on him all his life. This is him taking it back," she said before looking at me.

"Come on, baby. Fight back!" she yelled at me. I could feel myself getting sleepy, and I didn't want that. Although I arranged with my boys to kill my dad if he managed to take me out, I didn't want to give up. My eyes fell on Kaliyah, and everything we had ever been through flashed through my head. My mama had shown me the photograph with Kaliyah and me as babies. I always felt like that night I found her, our paths were destined to cross. I just didn't know that destiny had been written from the womb.

We locked eyes, and I felt comfort knowing that her face would be the last thing that I saw. Then, my anger took over. I wasn't done looking at her face just yet or making that family my pops stole from me. If I closed my eyes and went to sleep, I was making that motherfucker win.

I quickly looked around at the faces around me. Each and every one of them needed me, and I needed them, so tapping out wasn't an option! Somehow, I found the strength to pull my pop's arms from around my neck. I wrestled out from underneath him and rolled my body over his until I was now on his back. I gripped him around his neck with my arm and pulled it tight, putting as much pressure as I could to his neck. He tried to pull my arms away, but his strength had left his body by that point. I squeezed and squeezed gritting my teeth.

"Rest in peace, motherfucker."

I said my signature farewell when I was about to kill someone before using brute strength. I snapped his neck. We were on our knees, so when his body fell forward, I went with him and collapsed on his back, breathing hard. I felt little hands on me, and I looked up to see Kaliyah looking at me with tears running down her face. I pulled her into my arms and kissed all over her face.

"That night I found you, I made a promise to always protect you, and I meant that shit… even if it was against my own pops," I told her, and she nodded her head yes.

I looked down at my dad's dead body and surprisingly, I

didn't feel a damn thing. That nigga allowed greed and jealousy to lead him, and that cost him his life. I looked at Optimus and gave him the go ahead to call Trevor to come and clean up this place.

Standing to my feet with the help of Kaliyah, my mama grabbed me into a tight hug and kissed my sore face.

"I'm sorry you had to do that, baby. He was a bastard, but he was still your father," she said, and I nodded.

"All I need is you, mama, and I'm good." "Now what?" Django asked.

"This king is about to take some time out with my queen, and then we can talk," I said, limping my fucked up ass out of the warehouse.

"I'm driving," Crew yelled out, following behind me. I pulled Kaliyah into my arms and took my queen home!

Chapter Twenty – Nine

Kaliyah Johnson – Jones

IF A YEAR AGO SOMEONE WOULD HAVE told me that I was going to be a rich woman with a king for a husband, I would have laughed in their face! A young broken girl who came from a house of abuse who not even her own mother could love would find a man to love her? Yeah, right.

Here I stood, living that very life. It had been a few weeks since everything went down, and I found out who my father was. The events of Mr. Jones were behind us, and everyone was putting their lives back together.

Deshaun decided to give back the business his father stole and took by force. We didn't want to be associated with anything that Pattison had. Those families were happy to take their empires back and still decided to give Deshaun a portion of their profits, even though he told them they didn't have to. I think everyone was just happy to be rid of Pattison.

Being in the position I was in, I was able to see first-hand of what he was really like, and he wasn't a very nice man. He had women who he made give him sex in exchange for sparing their husbands' lives. People like Django who had to pay a protection fee to Pattison were now finally free to spend their money on what they wanted to. As for the streets with the dope and other things that Deshaun was directly involved with, he decided to put Crew in charge of the whole operation with Optimus, Demon, and Goliath as lieutenants.

As he promised, Chicken's family in Jamaica received money on his behalf and would continue to do so every month. Mrs. Jones was no longer walking around with a dark cloud over her head. She was the happiest Deshaun had ever seen her, and I was happy for her.

Life as I knew it on this part was good… better than good! For the first time, I was happy mentally, emotionally, and physically. Using some of the money my pops left for me, I opened a center for people like me who may have been abused or who had parents on drugs. It was a safe haven for them to talk to someone, do homework, or just chill out when they felt like they couldn't go home. It had rooms too and housed a few ran away teens.

I hired some excellent therapists, and I worked there too, motivating young people with my life story. Even Pedra worked there with her crazy ass. She was actually good with the people who went there, and a lot of them found it easy talking to her about things that were going on at home. Next door, I also set up a program for those parents who wanted to get off the drugs and take parenting courses to learn how to build a bond again with their children.

It was a success, and I couldn't have asked for any more. I had morphed into a woman and used all the pain I endured to build myself up. Of course, I didn't do it alone. Deshaun was my everything. He truly was my rib, and God knew what he was doing when he made our paths re-cross on that unforgettable night.

As for my family, Zoe emailed to tell me that she was getting sexually abused by one of the workers there, and whenever she would tell anyone, they wouldn't believe her and call her crazy. I didn't want to say good, but I knew that was her karma. She did some things to me that I would never forget, and for that, I couldn't have any sympathy for her. I wasn't sure what had happened to her since she sent that email a few weeks ago, because I didn't respond, and after that, I stopped using that email. There was no reason for me to continue any connection with that part of my past.

My uncle was doing okay in jail. He was given five years. Due to him giving himself up and the fact that my mama was the one who got him strung out on the mess in the first place, Deshaun pulled some strings and made it be put on his file that he was in there for fraud. If the real reason was ever discovered, he would have been targeted and killed. Although he hurt me, I didn't want that for him, especially as he had no control over it. He had plans to go back to Boston once his bid was done, and I was happy for him. We probably would never see each other again or talk for that matter, but I wished him well.

Oh, and I know you must be wondering about my mama! The last I heard, she almost died from an overdose after her pimp fed her too much coke. I would have thought that a near death experience would have made her come to her senses and stop with the drugs, but the day she was released from the hospital, the next night she was entertaining men at a house party. I only knew this because the streets talked, even all the way from Europe where she found herself shipped to. Her hate for me didn't subside, and somehow, she blamed me for her getting caught by traffickers. I guess some things will never change!

Goldie and Silvan were a distant memory, and their names were never mentioned.

I looked in the mirror, and I could barely recognize myself. The Kaliyah now was not the same Kaliyah who ran away almost a year ago. This Kaliyah had confidence, wore a smile on her face, a little makeup, and showed skin on a body that my husband couldn't keep his hands or mouth off.

"What you in the mirror smiling and looking all creepy for?" Deshaun laughed as he walked into the room. "Creepy nigga is my thing. Don't be stealing my shit," he said, making me laugh.

"Something is wrong with you, Deshaun."

"Yeah, it's called pussy whipped by my wife," he laughed, and I sucked my teeth at him.

"You made a nigga lose his mind with that lethal shit between yo' legs," he grabbed my ass and tried to grab my pussy, but I pushed him away.

"Come on now, baby. We need to get it in making Grim junior," he said, pulling me into his arms and picking me up. When he dropped me down on the bed, he said, "Look, I saved you from walking," and smiled.

Laughing, I said, "Oh, my hero."

He pulled my legs and dragged me to the end of the bed toward him. Taking my clothes off and then his, he positioned himself at my opening and pushed his way into me.

"Nah, baby... I'm your *knight in street king armor.*"

He smiled and kissed me as he skillfully wound his hips into me, hitting my spot instantly.

"You ain't ever lied!" I said, wrapping my arms and legs around my king.

The End

CPSIA information can be obtained
at www.ICGtesting.com
Printed in the USA
LVOW11s0017260717

542602LV00001BA/121/P

9 781548 317737